RESURRECTION

ZED AMADEO

SCIENCE FICTION FANTASY
FOR THE CULTURE
W.CLARK PUBLISHING

Wahida Clark Presents Innovative Publishing
60 Evergreen Place
Suite 904A
East Orange, New Jersey 07018
1(866) 910-6920
www.wclarkpublishing.com

Library of Congress Cataloging-In-Publication Data:
Resurrection
978-1-954161-54-2 Paperback
978-1-954161-53-5 Hardback
978-1-954161-71-9 eBook
978-1-954161-55-9 Audiobook
LCCN: 2021916358

1. Horror Fiction Novels 2. Characters with Anxiety 3. Magical Realism Fiction 4. Dark Contemporary Fantasy 5. Books about Magic Training 6. Stories about Magic Worlds 7. Magical Beings 8. Magical Best Friend 9. Stories about Learning Magic 10. Paranormal and Urban Stories
Creative Direction by Nuance Art LLC
Cover design by Tina Shivers
Layout by Caroline Zonis
Printed in United States

To all spooky women everywhere.

ACKNOWLEDGMENTS

First, I want to thank my mom and dad for always being my biggest cheerleaders. You nurtured my storytelling from the beginning. Thank you to my family for your support.

I want to thank the entire team at WCP and SF/F for believing in my writing enough to make this book possible. Wahida, Chase, D.B. and Deb – you inspire me to keep at it and I truly cannot thank the team enough for helping me bring my writing dreams to reality.

Thank you to Z for reading an early draft of this story many years ago and giving me the feedback that pushed me to self-publish the first version of this story.

I also want to give a shout out to those who read the self-published version of Kindred back in 2015. Thank you for your enthusiasm and excitement for my new fictional world.

For the inspiration and spark behind this story, I want to thank the SCP Community, David Mitchell, and Mark Z. Danielewski, for creating such amazing, boundary-defying fiction that inspired me to push my creativity further than I ever thought possible.

In August of 2018, during a personal creative drought, I

attended a writing conference. I want to thank the other genre writers I met there, and the amazing conference speakers, for their support and successes that rekindled my creativity during a time when I really doubted myself.

And finally, thank you, reader, for giving my storytelling a chance.

1

Pain. Blood. Darkness. I wanted to let it all slip away, let the torture ease into nothingness. I would've given anything not to exist.

Was I safe now? I didn't feel safe; I hurt like hell and I couldn't shake the pervading sense of terror that clung to me like a second skin.

I was being pushed through a hallway with bright lights above me. Each breath, gurgling with blood, was excruciating. I closed my eyes and found myself in a different room when I opened them. People in surgical masks hovered above me. Their scrubs were covered in blood. My blood?

Were they here to help me?

Nothing could touch my skin without bringing nauseating pain, like being cooked alive with no heat. I wanted to yell, but all I could let out was the smallest trickle of breath. The frozen scream remained stuck in my shattered throat; my lips were paralyzed in a rictus of agony.

~

I SHOULDN'T HAVE BEEN OUT ALONE in the state I was in. But I had driven tipsy before, and nothing ever happened. The suburban area I was driving from hardly had anyone on the road, anyway. When I felt my eyelids lower, I pulled over to the closest source of light I could find. That little strip mall would have to do, even if two of the stores looked like they had been abandoned for years. I pulled into an empty parking spot in front of a busted old liquor store for a moment to recharge and let my card idle.

A friend had once told me nothing good happened after 4:00 A.M. and you might as well just head off to bed. I fought a yawn as I unbuckled my seat belt and checked my cell. No new messages. The latest one had been from my sister, Kayla, about 20 minutes ago when she asked what time I was coming home. She threw an impromptu party at the little house we shared. She invited some friends she met through her acting gigs and wanted me to join. I couldn't pass up the opportunity to connect with other people who performed some kind of art. You never know when you might run into someone who would be the missing link to shoot you to stardom. That was what kept me going through my dull, pointless office job; my dream that one day I would be able to share my voice with the world was my fuel for living. I would show everyone my true worth, even if I wasn't as glamorous as Kayla no matter how hard I tried.

A place like this strip mall during the day usually wasn't an issue. Now that it was well into the twilight hours between night and day, I double-checked the locks on my doors just in case. I looked around to make sure I was alone. I had read the articles about the recent crime wave, the increase in unsolved murders and thefts occurring for little to no reason at all. But I had no need to worry about that. Not in the little world I lived in at the time.

When I looked down again to check for messages on my phone, I saw movement out the corner of my eye.

I jerked my head forward to look through the windshield. I thought I imagined the two floating dots in the distance, zooming across the night sky like shooting stars with their own agenda, chasing each other back and forth. The longer I stared, the more defined they became, until I was certain these moving shapes were not figments of my imagination. The pull of curiosity and confusion kept me glued to my seat, staring up at the sky. My pulse raced somewhere between fear and exhilaration.

As the shapes drew closer and my disbelief grew, I realized they weren't just dots. They were people. *People. People flying!* At that range, I could make out the vulgar names they were calling each other, goading each other on. I blinked and rubbed my eyes. *This couldn't be happening.*

When I looked back up, they were still zipping across the sky. Soon they were flying right over the strip mall, close enough for me to see the young, masculine faces and the objects between their legs - long, bumpy staffs like the roughhewn pole of a broomstick. Suddenly, it didn't matter how *impossible* this was - if I was close enough to make out that much detail, that meant they were close enough to see me. Heart suddenly thudding in my chest, I ducked down into my seat and pulled the key out of the ignition to turn my car off before they heard the engine.

I tried to duck down more, hoping to get out of sight. But before I could, one of them saw me and pointed me out to his companion. They both froze in mid-air, staring down at me, sending my heart racing to my throat.

"I think she can *see* us," one of them said.

"She can," the second one said, smiling. "She can see us." *What did they mean by that?* We were in clear view of each other.

They moved in closer and flew straight toward my windshield, hovering just above my car, and banged on my windows with their fists. My stomach lurched, giving me the sensation I was about to throw up. I screamed, struggling to open my door, and stumbled onto the concrete. My party heels and dress made any movement difficult and almost impossible for me to run away. I turned in the direction of the parking lot, yelling for help, but I could not see or hear anyone nearby, not even a car. As I stood and looked for refuge, something behind me knocked me flat on my stomach. Winded and too terrified to move, my mind scrambled for solutions that wouldn't come.

Somewhere from behind, the two men laughed. When I looked back, I saw that they were too far away to have knocked me over. My thoughts raced for a logical explanation. What could have done that?

Soon, their laughter was right above me.

I struggled to pull myself together before making another attempt toward safety. Suddenly, something gripped my body. It felt like a massive hand holding me in place. My mind gibbered that this couldn't be happening. I looked down, expecting to see a rope, giant man, tentacle monster, or *something*. I was disappointed when all I saw was my dress. *My super cute party dress I may or may not have borrowed without permission.* I was in paralyzing shock as something rolled me over, forcing me onto my back. It was like there was a third person that I couldn't see who was causing all of this. My eyes raced from one direction to another, searching for something in the men's hands, anything that could have caused what I was experiencing. If I could find something concrete, maybe I could save myself and make it out of there alive.

It was like my mind refused to accept the absurd scene in front of me. Two men flying? This couldn't be real. I had to be trapped in a nightmare. But the chill spreading through my veins told me that I was very much awake.

The two hovered on both sides of me.

"How can she see us?" the first one asked, talking about me as if I wasn't lying helplessly beneath them.

"I really don't know," the second said. "Guess that invisibility spell wasn't so long-lasting. Wore off a lot sooner than it was supposed to, didn't it?"

"I am gonna kick Greg's ass for that next time we see him. What a scam." The first one turned toward me.

"What's your name?" he asked. I couldn't stop my lips from trembling long enough to give him an answer.

"What's your name?" he repeated louder.

"D- Dina," I mumbled. My name somehow stumbled out of my mouth involuntarily. My mind snapped back into reality, somehow accepting the impossible for the moment. All I could think of was that I didn't want to die. No matter how ridiculous this was, maybe if I played along, after whatever they had planned for me, they would let me go. I didn't want to be another dead body disposed of like trash.

"Well then, Dina, we're going to have some fun with you tonight." They reached for my arms and hoisted me up into the air between them as they ascended, my stomach doing somersaults. I had to find a way out of there.

"Please, just let me go!" I cried, flailing my legs. "Please!"

The more I screamed, the more they laughed.

They finally released me while flying over a patch of grass. My body thudded against the ground. Even cushioned by the lush, springy grass, the fall still hurt. As I groaned in pain, they descended, dropping their flying sticks, and walked over to me. Something took control of me again, uncurling my body against my will, leaving me vulnerable before them. I kept still this time. I couldn't fight back against something I couldn't see.

The first one laughed as he walked toward me, extending his arm as if he was going to touch me, but he never did. I somehow found myself an inch off the ground, scrambling with my fingers to anchor myself to the grass. I couldn't believe it. I was levitating. *What the hell had I stumbled into? What were they going to do to me?*

For a moment, I dangled in the air, fearful of falling at any moment. I kept myself quiet as if the silence would protect me from whatever was going to happen next. My stomach jolted when I was dropped back onto the ground. My face crashed against the dirt and stone, which sent tremors like an earthquake through my head. The metallic taste and scent of blood filled my mouth and nose. When I inhaled, sharp pangs ran through my chest.

Somehow, I was floating again. I thrust out my arms below me to try to soften the blow, but it made no difference. My ears rang with each smash against the ground and the blood poured down my face. I crashed against the ground again. And again. And again, until I suddenly realized that I wasn't moving. He must have stopped. Maybe he was gone.

I rolled over onto my back, grunting with each movement and exhausting myself. My lungs needed oxygen, but my body ached with each breath. Although I was still, the trees, grass, and sky all looked like they were spinning around me. I saw the world through a red sheen, as blood and sweat pooled in my eyes. I had always viewed the term "scared to death" with skepticism, but there I was, so afraid I expect my heart to stop.

I heard them before I saw them. Even with the loud ringing echoing through my head, I still could hear the first one laughing. My heart dropped. They still weren't done.

"Your turn," he said to the second one. I didn't have the energy to move or to endure the inevitable pain that I would experience trying to escape. He stepped toward me and came back into my field of vision, muttering words I couldn't understand. I heard what sounded like a match being lit. The air grew unbearably hot, until it felt like I was on the surface on the sun. The skin on my arms began to blister.

My vision went black before I could see it, and I was engulfed.

Every part of me had been set ablaze. I had descended into a new world of pain.

The smoky smell of my own flesh burning incinerated my lungs. I couldn't breathe. The torment made it impossible for me to feel my limbs. Nothing existed beyond the fire that was going to kill me and the scream that filled my head.

Without warning, the temperature dropped. I took in a big gulp of non-smoky air and opened my eyes, expecting to find myself surrounded by fire. Instead, I was still lying on the grass with the first man standing in front of me. There wasn't any smoke. No ash. My "burnt" arms were bloody but not blistered. I didn't understand. How was this happening? There wasn't a fire. I hadn't gone anywhere.

But I was still alive.

"This one's tough," the second one said. "The other ones would've surely been dead by now." I took in sharp, shallow breaths while the momentary relief shifted back into panic.

"You know what that means," the first one said. "Time for the real fun to begin."

That was the only chance I was going to get to potentially save myself while they were talking. I bit my bloody lip and tried to gather whatever willpower I had left. Maybe I could crawl away and hide. When I stretched out my right arm, something cracked and the rest of my body seized up, betraying me. I screamed out in pain.

Someone's fingers were suddenly running through my hair, forcing my head up.

"Don't try that again," the first one said. He shoved my face back into the ground. A sickening crunch echoed in my head and more blood poured down my face. The flood of panic set in when I realized that I couldn't fight back. I could hardly force myself to move. It didn't matter what I did. They were going to kill me. I wasn't going to get out alive.

I did not try to fight back.

"I think she deserves a punishment," the first one said. "What do you think, Joe?"

"I think you're right," Joe said.

"I'll handle this one," the still nameless first one said.

I couldn't struggle against it, could hardly even scream. Something worse was about to happen. Yet, I was powerless to stop it. The nameless one wore the vilest grin as he kneeled next to me, blocking out the little light and comfort the moon and stars were giving me.

Joe tore the remains of my dress from my body, taking away my final shield. With a knife outstretched in his hand, Joe walked in a quick circle around us and then stood by Nameless's side. He then handed Nameless another knife he pulled from his cloak. I stared at Joe, wanting to plead with him to help me, but I couldn't. All I could do was let the tears well in my eyes, washing away the blood and dirt, waiting for it all to be over. I cried as Nameless pierced the already broken flesh on my stomach with the knife's sharp edge as both he and Joe whispered in an unknown language. My bare body trembled. This was it. This was the end for me.

They turned around as if they were about to walk away.

Maybe the nightmare was finally ending. My body was bruised and broken, but I was going to live, if I could hold on just a little bit longer.

My heart dropped when they turned around and came back toward me, holding handfuls of stones.

"You must know that in our world, there is only one punishment for trespassing: death. Consider this as a lesson to your kind," Nameless said. I tried to shake my head, unable to speak. I wanted to beg them, plead with them not to do this. They could just let me go and I wouldn't tell anyone. Not a single soul. I opened my bloody mouth to try to speak, but nothing came out.

One stone after another crashed into my naked body, shattering what little part of me remained. All that existed to me was the agony pulsing from one part of my body to another. I was tired of trying to hold on. I just wanted to let go.

"It was nice knowing you, Dina," Nameless said.

I was paralyzed as they walked away again, picking up the wooden staffs they discarded previously. My head slumped to the side as they flew away and disappeared from my view. Their laughter became distant until I couldn't hear them anymore.

My body was outstretched, defiled, and broken like my mind. I should have been able to move again. They were gone. A voice in my head reminded me that I could get away now, look for help. Yet no part of me was eager or able to move even an inch. The unbearable pain throbbed through every part of me. All I could do was stare at the ground, stained with puddles of my blood, until my eyes filmed over and even the grass seemed to disappear.

2

Someone disturbed my comfortable darkness, awakening me back into a world of pain. I wanted to return to my internal cocoon. Anything to block the flood of memories that unconsciousness kept at bay. Disappear into a reality where this impossible agony did not exist. My eyes flew open at the sound of a person nearby, then my world became painfully bright. I struggled to focus on the finer details of what was around me.

I was surrounded by a crowd of indistinct people. Someone was interrupting my unnatural sleep, saying something I couldn't understand. Someone else was throwing up in the distance. One person was pacing back and forth on their phone. Another was asking for my name. A stranger laid their coat over me. I appreciated the thought behind the kind deed, but the mere touch of soft fabric on any part of my broken body was enough to send me into another fit of pain I couldn't voice. I wanted to return to my land of darkness where no pain existed. This world had too many sensations. Instead of screaming, I only released a sigh as my mind faded out of focus.

I drifted in and out too many times to count, always wishing to slip away again as soon as I awakened. The next thing I knew, I found myself in a sterile white hospital room, covered with bandages and needles in my arms. The nurses, doctors, and police seemed to speak in slow motion, as if I were trapped in a dream-like state. My body was at last numb from the inescapable torment. They wanted me to recall what happened to me; to relive what I was already trying to escape. They managed to dull my body from the pain only to provoke suffering again in my mind. All I could see were the faces of those men full of sickening glee as they destroyed my body. I had flashes of their insults, the pain, the strangeness, drowning out most of what was happening to me in the present. It was all a trick; a game I couldn't win. My lips felt numb as I spoke. My words left my mouth like foreign objects. I couldn't be sure any of my answers to their questions made sense. Why couldn't they just leave me alone to return to my world of emptiness?

Days later, I was released from that sterile prison. I was on so many painkillers that everything around me was hazy. Kayla kept me propped up as I stumbled into the house, only to find another small crowd in the form of family members sitting inside the living room. I couldn't handle more people asking me questions, staring at me with faces of heavy concern. This wasn't a situation any of them were equipped to handle. I don't know what Kayla said to them, but they left me in peace as she helped me into my bedroom.

My bed was covered with *Get Well* cards, flowers, and candy, none of which I could appreciate in my current mental state. Kayla cleared the bed off for me and helped me lie down. I sank into the soft mattress and looked up at my sister while she rearranged my pillows. I found myself sinking deeper into a pit of memories. Reliving my trauma, as if it was the only thing that was real. The strip mall. The men. All the impossible things I had somehow witnessed. The knowledge that no matter how long it took for my scars to heal, I already knew my life would never return to the way it once was.

"They were flying," I said, the words falling out of my mouth as I struggled to create each sound. "They moved me with their minds."

Kayla turned her face away from the pillows and toward me; her brow furrowed in confusion.

"They're never going to be found," I said. Kayla opened her mouth slightly but did not say a word. I didn't care. Life was not a script; it was a nightmare. There were things nobody would understand. *They'll call me crazy.* I couldn't stop.

With the first trickle of ideas slipping from my lips, I couldn't keep my thoughts inside anymore.

I told Kayla everything, even the details I neglected to tell the police when they paid me a visit in the hospital. I couldn't tell whether she understood me with my dry mouth and murky mind, but that didn't matter as much as getting my story out to someone. My sister was the person I could trust the most in this world.

When my words trickled off into a stammering of random syllables, I finally gave up trying to explain my current state of mind. She waited until I fell silent to respond by shaking her head. I wished I'd kept everything to myself and gave her the story I told the police.

"Dina," she said, laying a hand on my arm, and looking at my face with wide eyes. "Get some rest, okay? You're home now." She kissed my forehead and left the room. My body shook after having unleashed what I was forced to keep inside, and then gushes of tears were freed from my eyes.

My sister came back and smoothed my hair back before handing me a smoothie with a straw. She took my hand and cupped it around the glass, helping me slip the straw between my shaking lips.

"I'm asking everyone to leave soon," she said. "We'll have the house back to ourselves. Just call if you need anything. Alright, Dina? I'm here for you. We're going to get through this together." I saw a sparkle in her eyes, tears that she too was afraid to let loose before she left again.

I looked down at my pink smoothie, barely able to stomach the liquid. My stomach convulsed, so I set it down.

My reflection in the full-length mirror caught my eye, giving me a first good look at my damaged body that I hardly recognized. My face was engorged with patches of purple and red bruises. The parts of me my clothes left exposed were covered with white and pink-stained bandages. Below the bandages, invisible to the mirror but clear in my mind, was the strange symbol of a triangle within a circle etched on my stomach. Of all my injuries, I wanted that one to scab over and heal so I could forget it had ever been there.

Although my sister's room was close to mine, I was alone, enclosed within my own four walls in the dark that kept me pinned down and paralyzed in my bed. I replayed that night repeatedly, begging for it all to come to an end as my eyes released endless rivers of tears. Memories of those two men had already embedded themselves into my mind. What if they came back to finish what they had started? They could be outside of the window right now, hiding in the shadows. The dark shapes I thought to be tree branches, waving in the wind, could be them descending from the sky, preparing to enter my house. Kayla couldn't protect me from them; not even the authorities could. No one could keep me safe from the mysterious powers they possessed. I couldn't protect myself in my current state. I was powerless. Even if a thousand people came to my defense, *I'd only create a thousand victims.*

When I wailed out in the middle of the night, unable to sleep for my racing thoughts. Kayla came running into my room. This time, her usual words didn't comfort me. Even my world of darkness, the peace promised by sleep, seemed too far off in the distance for me to ever reach.

3
___

Kayla didn't think I could hear her loud whispers as she spoke with our parents in the living room. She must have thought I was sleeping or simply too out of it to pay attention.

"I'm really worried about Dina," she said. Her words were muffled through the wall but still understandable.

"We all are," our mother responded. "I can't even imagine what she's going through right now. The most we can do is be there for her when she needs us, right?"

"No, it's beyond that. When she spoke to me the night that she came home...she wasn't making sense," Kayla said.

"What do you mean?" our father asked. "Maybe it was just the pain medicine. Remember that time when I hurt my arm? I don't think I was making much sense either for the first couple of weeks afterward."

"I don't think that's it. She started telling me things about what had happened to her that night," Kayla said. There was a moment of silence as if my family were grieving for my loss.

"Like what? Is this anything that we should go to the police about?" our mother asked. I wanted to run into the living room and beg her to keep what I had told her confidential. She didn't deserve to know anything if this was what she would do with my trust.

"No, like I said, she wasn't making sense," she said. "She started talking about how they were...I can't even believe that I'm saying this, but she said that they were flying. And that they used their minds to move her or something." I pictured Kayla shaking her head, even stifling a laugh, as if this was a ridiculous sitcom scenario and not the worst thing to ever happen to me.

"Well, Kayla, she could be having a difficult time understanding what happened to her. I think that I've heard of things like this happening to other people after a traumatic event. She probably needs to speak with someone," our mother said.

"Maybe. I hope. I just don't know what to do. It's just the two of us, you know? And I'm not sure if I'm who she really needs right now. I'm not sure if I'm equipped to handle this."

"Of course not. You're not a doctor, Kayla. That's who she really needs to see."

"All I know is that if I can get my hands on the men that did this to her..." my father began, and trailed off into silence.

"I'm not sure how to talk to her anymore," Kayla said.

"Don't worry about it, Kayla. We can talk to her tonight about what she might need," our mother said.

My parents stopped by my room later in the evening. My mother sat on the edge of my bed, taking one of my hands into hers, while my father pulled up a chair beside us. He stared at the ground, as if he couldn't bear to look at me in my current state. After asking me the usual questions about how I was feeling and whether I needed anything, my mother took in a deep breath and squeezed my hand tighter. I could feel a revelation or question about to force its way out from between her lips.

"Kayla's been taking good care of you, hasn't she?" she asked. *Of course she is,* I thought to myself, *like the responsible older sister that she is.* I nodded.

"I'm so happy that you have her right now," she said, then paused slightly. "But Kayla can't do this all on her own."

"What do you mean?" I asked. After overhearing her conversation earlier, I knew exactly what she meant, but I wanted to hear her say it.

"It's just that-"

"Kayla isn't a doctor, Dina," my father chimed in. My mother cast her face down as he spoke. "She told us about some of the things that you were saying. None of us here can imagine what you are going through right now. We can't help you the way that you need it right now. We know that you're still healing, but you need to talk to someone who can help you through this."

"Someone like who?" I asked.

"You need to see a professional, Dina," my father said. "A therapist. We will pay for it, obviously. Your doctor even recommended it right before you came home. And we really think that it's best."

I could see where they were coming from. They were right in that they had no idea of what I was going through right now, how torturous being awake and even asleep often was for me. How I couldn't escape from the memories that continued to pin me down. The pain from the injuries was nothing compared to that kind of agony. At least I could take a pill to temporarily dull my body. Not even the pain pills were enough to slow down my mind. But what kind of therapist would take me seriously or consider my story to be anything beyond a coping mechanism, especially when my own sister didn't even believe me? I would only be able to tell them false stories. My body filled with heat. My already sore muscles tensed at the thought of facing more disbelief over what I knew was impossible, yet true. No one would believe my story. My eyes pooled with tears.

"Dina, what's wrong?" my mother asked. She reached up to wipe the tears trailing down my face. "We really think that this could be a good opportunity for you. We just want the best for you, and we don't know that Kayla is what you need right now." I could describe to them the thoughts that ran through my mind when they made their suggestion, but chances were they wouldn't care much. My mother leaned into me, and my father got up from his seat to wrap his arms around both of us.

Even with all members of my closest family under one roof, I felt alone, unsafe and unheard.

4

______

I was suffocating beneath it all. The looping memories of that night, my mind wandering down all the different steps I could have taken to change what happened to me, to make it into an ordinary Saturday night again. If only I hadn't gone to that stupid mall. I could have driven off as soon as I saw those dots in the sky, before the men had the chance to see me. I could have stayed home from the start, not going out to that party in the first place. What had been the decision that sealed my fate? Of all the places where I could have been that night, what did I do to cross paths with those men?

Whatever the decision was, I didn't make it. The night played out before me as I sat in my car, watching them fly, knowing what was about to happen to me next, but powerless to change the past. The agony coursing through my body again as they tortured me in mysterious ways, digging into my flesh, destroying my mind. I gave up trying to fight against the recollections. They were now all that seemed to matter.

My bedroom should have been the only place I felt safe, but it became my prison. The only time I left my room was when

Kayla took me to the doctor to check on the progress of my physical wounds followed by additional encouragement for me to seek a therapist for my mental ones. My answer to that suggestion remained the same as it had always been. Silence. I could try to explain my reasons why, but no one would believe the truth.

I retreated into myself, allowing my bed-ridden hours to blur into each other. The only thing to mark the passing of time were the changes in my wounds, and bandages removed from certain parts of my body. The once fresh injuries were now dulled into dark scars. I couldn't avoid the symbols on my abdomen. Whenever I undressed for a shower, wounds remained red despite the time that passed. The bodily damage would never fade; it was a reminder of the strange and impossible things I saw. Concrete evidence of what happened to me was more unusual than anyone else would want to believe. For the longest time, I had nothing besides my memories and those scars as proof of what happened to me instead of the story everyone else would want me to believe.

When Kayla came into my room to check on me, she tended to leave my window open to let in some fresh air. The sounds of the outside world just beyond my window became one of my few sources of focus outside of my crushing memories. The wind blowing, trees swaying back and forth, cars passing by, and indistinguishable chatter were reminders there still was an outside world even if I was trapped inside. I closed my eyes sometimes and let the outside sounds fill my half-asleep, half-awake mind for as long as I could before the inevitable loops returned to destroy my brief moments of peace. An outside world did exist, but I was no longer a part of it, and no part of it seemed eager for me to return.

A small shadow flitted past my window one night, breaking up the monotony of what I usually saw while staring at the window, the barrier between me and the outside world. I figured it was nothing but a large bug. The shape slipped into my room through the open space in the window, flying through my room until it settled on my desk on the opposite side of my room. It was close enough to no longer be a vague shadow, visible in the moonlight that trickled through my window. The tiny blue creature that flew into my bedroom had two tiny wings as dark as the rest of its humanoid body. Whatever this thing was, it wasn't a bug. While I stared at yet another impossible thing that had somehow entered my life, it jerked its head toward me, revealing a face without eyes or a nose. It only had a small line that stretched across the lower half of its face like a closed mouth.

I should have considered the possibility I was hallucinating or at least having a waking dream. I could have screamed out for Kayla to figure out whether she could see this creature or it was a figment of my imagination. I could have bolted from my room to escape from another bizarre incident in my life that could mean danger. Though my breath quickened in my chest and my heart raced faster than I could remember since I came home, I extended my right arm slowly to reach toward it. I didn't want to run away or fight anymore. I needed to know what this thing was, what it meant, and why this was happening to me. I needed to know what I was seeing was real.

It could have disappeared entirely if it had been a figment of my imagination or flew away through the window. Instead, it moved its wings and flew toward me, settling into my palm and looking at me with its eyeless face. When I lowered my arm to rest beside me, the creature did not move an inch.

Whatever this was, I could feel its weight and texture as it sat in my hand. No one could accuse me of being crazy. This thing, this creature, was real, even if it came from the realm of the impossible. The creature sat pointed toward me, as if it were interested in me. It was the first being in a long while to give me that feeling.

"What are you?" I asked it. Though it didn't or couldn't respond, it tilted its head as if curious for me to continue.

"I'm Dina," I said. "I know you can't be real, but here you are." The creature moved its wings around, tickling my palm before falling still again.

"I can't believe that you're here. No one else would believe what I'm seeing right now. Not even my sister. I can hardly believe that this is happening. But you're certainly real, aren't you?" It nodded its small head; its first direct response to anything that I had said so far. This creature was the first real ear I'd had in a while that would listen to what I had to say.

"Do you know how much it hurts being here? I want to get away from all of this." It continued to *look* at me, remaining still in my palm.

"I don't know why I'm even talking to you. I don't know what you are or where you came from. But you seem friendly enough. You know, you're the first to really listen to me in a long time," I said. It remained silent.

"Thank you for listening." The creature bowed its head before flitting away through that same crack in the window, leaving no trace of its visit behind.

Another mysterious force entered my life, leaving just as quickly as it arrived. A creature with uncertain origins should have terrified me, but it made me question my sanity and reality. *What is real anyway?* This was a good thing, *wasn't it?* More proof that what happened to me was unusual despite what anyone else would want me to believe. Even if this new force, this new creature, was strange and could very well wish me harm, it gave me my only moment of companionship, if only for a moment.

I didn't understand what just happened, nor did I have the

energy to untangle it. But I did fall into the longest, deepest sleep I'd had since my life had been twisted into an acid trip.

I STARED at my window for hours on end, waiting for the strange critter to return. When it flitted through my open window again a few days later, I held my arm out immediately, calling it over once more. It flew over again and took its place in my hand, its face pointed toward me, giving me the sense it was still staring at me even without eyes.

"Thank you for coming back," I said. "You have no idea how much I appreciate you returning," I said, happy to see the little critter. More and more I felt like my family was crazy for not listening to me. For not wanting to know. This little blue *whatever it is,* actually listened and that made it an ally. The line on the lower half of its face stretched wider, as if that were its mouth.

"Why are you here? What do you want?" It raised a thin arm and pointed to one of the gift boxes of chocolates I received from a family member on my dresser. I nodded, and the creature flitted over, prying the cover off and heaving a candy into a mouth that had suddenly revealed itself. The hole in its face that appeared after it widened the line on its face. As it opened its mouth to take a bite, a mouth full of tiny, razor-sharp teeth were revealed that sunk into the chocolate. When it finished, it hovered back toward me, heaving to and from as if it was full before plopping down into my hand, staring up at me as if waiting for me to continue the conversation. Sometimes I sang to it, humming a tune I once practiced during my vocal lessons, or an old song from a high school chorus performance; the only time I felt within my element. The only place where I felt I belonged.

So, our ritual began every other night when it was too late to have any chance of being interrupted.

The first night I told it everything I couldn't tell Kayla or anyone else about the night I was attacked. The memories I struggled to keep from ruling my mind finally seeped out of me, telling the creature one true detail after the next as I trembled and exploded with tears from each revelation. Instead of flying away, or accusing me of being delusional, it sat there and continued to listen until I was too exhausted to continue. It slipped away beneath the window, somehow promising me it would return soon.

The next few nights, I told it of my life before any of this happened to me.

"You probably couldn't tell from the way that I look right now, but I used to just be Dina Durst, an aspiring actress, and an average blonde. The only reason I moved to Springfield was to follow in Kayla's footsteps. I can never seem to break out of her shadow, you know? Or maybe you don't know. I can't tell if you can even understand." It tilted its head again, which I took as an invitation to keep telling my story.

"Kayla always aced her classes and our parents never missed one of her plays when she was in high school. I was still living with our parents, waiting tables, not going anywhere when she moved to Springfield. That's when she started getting all these acting roles. Small ones, but still. I thought if I moved here, and took some more vocal lessons and lived with her, I would somehow mooch off her success and make my own career and finally be noticed. But no. I couldn't even land a stupid role in the broke down community theater musical. I'm still working at the same dead-end office job that I started out at. I might even lose that one too after this is all over. They might not even want me back after what has happened to me. Do you know what I learned from moving to this stupid city? There's no outshining Kayla. I do love her. She's my big sister after all. But I just wanted my chance in the spotlight, you know? I wanted our parents to come visit Springfield just so that they would see me. And now look at me. I'm bedridden and worse off than before. The only reason they come to visit now is because they feel sorry for me and think that I need to talk to a 'professional'. Like they're too afraid to say what they really mean. They think I'm crazy. They think I'm broken." I shook my head.

"I don't want them to be right." The creature leaned in and placed a tiny claw on my arm that I could hardly feel.

A tear ran down my cheek once I finally accepted that this was the only being in my life that would really listen to me was a creature whose existence made no sense inside the rules of my old reality. That little critter was my first taste into a reality that followed a different set of laws. *More than an ally, a friend.*

The creature returned a few nights later and we engaged in our normal nightly ritual. While it sat in my hand, I went on and on about the endless suggestions I received to go outside, talk to someone, and get some fresh air from the same people who disregarded my story. It sat and listened, flapping its wings from time to time. When I paused, it flew just above my hand, gently prodding me to flip my hand over with the palm facing down before grabbing my right index finger.

At first, I thought it wanted me to look in the direction it was making me point toward: the mirror on the opposite wall. In its reflection, I saw my body still partially covered with bandages to hide the wounds that stubbornly refused to heal.

"What is it? What do you want me to do?" It kept clutching my finger and jerking its head toward the mirror, toward the reflection that reminded me of everything I wanted to forget, like the strange dots moving across the sky. The destruction of my body as they ignored my screams and cries for help. Unable to take a step outside. Trapped in my room day after day, watching small pieces of the world float by my bedroom window. The pitiful tones my parents used when they spoke to me now. All that I could have been. Everything those two men had taken away from me. Joe and Nameless.

The heat from my anger rushed through me with each thought until I felt like I could burst and my vision ran red. The sharp noise of a crack released me from this cruel circle of remembrance.

The mirror broke.

5

______

"I need to figure it out," I told the creature one night. "I need to know why all of this is happening to me."

A handful of nights had passed since the incident in the mirror, a sight I couldn't forget. Right after it happened, I shooed the creature away back through my window. I looked back and forth at my hands and at the crack in the mirror, unable to comprehend the how or the why behind what I did. The creature never did anything like that before over the course of its visits. It had been encouraging me to do it, as if it needed to show me something important. Whenever I glanced over at my newly broken reflection, my heart raced and my face filled with a tingling warmth. I struggled to accept the fact I had done it. Part of me wanted to toss a sheet over the mirror and erase what happened from my mind. Escape from the connections it held with the worst thing that had ever happened to me. But I couldn't stop myself from staring at that crack in the glass, the mirror took the place of what my window had once been. I couldn't deny the sense of *power.*

The impossible had again became a part of my life. This time it wasn't outside of myself; an objective, terrifying evil that

27

was on the other side of the window. This time the impossible was something I created.

I could think of only one way I might be able to find an answer.

The little critter returned to me like a faithful pet that night, reassuring me that even if no one else wanted to listen to what I had to say, at least I had a strange buddy who would always return. It wanted to show me something before. The beginning of a change I previously had not been able to see. This odd animal was my only hope of figuring out where to go from here.

My fear wasn't going to hold me back. It nodded its head while it took a large bite out of the chocolate in its hands.

"Can you help me?" I asked as it perched on the top of my hand. It nodded and lifted itself up to hover in the air, flying toward my bedroom door.

I took in a deep breath and heaved my legs over the side of the bed. A million thoughts raced through my mind, conspiring to keep me in bed. Shouldn't I stay where I had been safe from the world outside? Shouldn't I remain in bed until I returned to normal, which might very well be never? After what I already experienced, I should be running away from the bizarre instead of straight toward it. Somehow, lying in bed for weeks hadn't kept the strange from trickling back into my life. The creature was a part of the force pushing me toward all of this. Pushing me toward a discovery. With all the strength I could muster in my weak and unused muscles, I pushed myself off the bed to stand.

My legs were shaky as I slid my feet into the slippers by my bed and walked toward the doorway. The creature hovered in the middle and faced me, guiding me with each step. It made motions for me to follow as it moved into the hallway and up to the front door, then floated in front of it. I froze before this final barrier. The last time I made this journey myself was the night before the attack, after I had spent hours trying to fix myself up to make a good impression with whoever I might've met at the party that night. I shouldn't go out tonight as well, following this creature into the unknown.

I imagined Joe and Nameless were coming toward me again, their faces full of frenzy, and me trapped with a panicked paralysis. If I stepped outside, I would no longer be as safe. They would come after me again to finish what they started, silencing me forever. *If not them, then someone else like them.* The casual cruelty of the attack had shaken me. Who knew what lurked out there, hidden in the shadows of the night, waiting for a vulnerable woman like me to wander into their trap. This all seemed like a terrible idea; the potential of danger was not worth fulfilling my curiosity.

The creature grabbed one of my fingers, yanking it toward the doorknob. I snatched my hand back. My breath rose and fell in my chest, my face flushed with heat.

"I can't," I told it. "Not yet."

It shook its head, again jerking my hand toward the door-knob. A spark of static ran through my hand as my skin made contact with the metal.

I could stay inside, trapped in a constant cocoon of fear and confusion while the days slipped away. I could let my life slide through my fingers. *It would be so easy.* I saw myself lying in my bed as weeks turned to months, and months passed into years until my blonde hair turned gray, my body withering to match the husk of a person I had become. I could be afraid until I was on my last breath. A wasted life, seventy years could pass with my core hardly any different from where I was right now. Or I could take a chance and take a step outside. Just one step. At the first sign of danger, I could always turn back around and return to the comfort of my sheets and pillows. I didn't know what awaited me in the world beyond, but I knew what would happen if I stayed here.

With one last deep breath, I wrapped my fingers around the

doorknob and made my entrance into the outside world. I took one hesitant step as I placed my right foot on the concrete. The creature continued to hover in front of me as I looked around in all directions, searching for anything that might be a sign of trouble. When all I saw was an ordinary, peaceful night, I took a step with my left foot. I had made it outside without Kayla's help. I let a sigh of relief loose, closing the door behind me. The creature flew forward, creating a new path for me to follow. Putting all my trust and safety into the hands of this mysterious creature, I shuffled behind it into the night.

I shadowed the creature down one path and then another. The tension in my body melted away with each step I took away from my old, stale sanctuary. When was the last time I had breathed in air this fresh? I walked down sidewalk after sidewalk, no soul in sight. My path was unknown, but I was at least free, if only for a little while.

As I continued along the path the creature led, a prickle of dread ran down my spine; the sensation increased with each step forward. This street, these buildings, this path was familiar. I had seen these sights from the corner of my eyes while I was being dragged along on a horrific trip against my will. I wanted to return home, but it seemed too late to stop now.

The realization of where the creature was leading me all along settled over me like a layer of fire. I put my trust into this thing and look where it had taken me. My confidence, my trust in the creature, my belief in my ability to overcome the injustice that broke my life, flew out of me at a rapid pace.

The patch of grass was wider than I remembered. This wasn't just a stray patch of green but a park in the middle of the city. Yet, I felt like everything around me was closing in until I could barely breath. A torrent of memories played out in front of me. Joe and Nameless were controlling me once again, beating me and destroying my body, digging into my skin with a blade until my lifeless body lost any spirit that remained.

I dropped to my knees, crying for my lost self those men took from me, losing the ability to control my balance until I flopped over face first into the ground. I couldn't move. I couldn't make myself leave the place that held such horrific memories.

Something tugged at my finger. I looked up to find it was the critter trying to get my attention again, making a hissing noise that I never heard it make before. Its head jerked toward the trees. Through blurry eyes, I caught a sliver of a sight through an opening in some of the trees I hadn't seen before. It was as if the scene was hidden from all spots in the trees except from my direction. Once I caught sight of what was going on, I could not pull myself away.

At first, all I could see from a distance was a swirl of color and peeks of people having a gathering in the forest; their loud chatter and laughter made its way over to me. I fought against the memories creeping back in and taking over my mind, pulling myself back up to stand. I took cautious steps forward until I reached the edge of the clearing. I stood behind a tree to conceal myself, taking in my new discovery.

I stumbled into a world that oversaturated my senses. The scene around me resembled a carnival set up in the middle of the forest, full of bright tents, crowds of people, and the pervasive smell of unknown food. This was where the creature had led me; the answers to my questions of what was happening to me. How I could suddenly gain the ability to break a mirror using my mind. I struggled to see how this provided the answers to my questions. Several of the people looked normal enough at first glance, but a second look tipped me off to the alien nature of this place. Several wore cloaks like what Joe and Nameless wore that night.

Whatever this place was, I knew I didn't belong. I could be in danger right now all because I decided to make the stupid decision of following this unknown creature through the dark.

I stumbled backward before turning my back to the gathering in the forest, preparing to make my exit out of there and keep the promise I made to myself earlier.

My heart flew into hysterics as I felt a tug at my shoulder much too forceful to be from the small hands of the creature, hovering in plain view in front of me.

"What are you doing here?" the raspy male voice asked me. Instead of turning around to view the voice's source, I took another step forward. I prepared to run as much as I could in my still injured state the first chance I got, but another hand gripped my other shoulder, pinning me in place.

"Did you hear me?" he asked again, now yelling. "I said, 'what are you doing here?'" With his tight grip on my shoulders, there was no way for me to get out of there just yet. I twisted my face to the side as much as I could to look him in the face.

"Nothing," I said. My lips trembled with every word. "I just want to leave." He forced me all the way around until I was looking at him. He looked me up and down, a sneer grew across his face.

"You're one of the *ayidi*, aren't you?" he asked. "An Ordinary. I can tell."

"I-I'm sorry! I just want to leave. Please!" I yelled.

"How did you end up here?" he shouted.

"I don't know!" I said, close to tears. "Please, just let me go." He shook his head.

"Do you know what we do to people like you? We can't just let you leave."

Before I could react, he put an arm around my waist and was dragging me away from where I stood, taking me farther into the middle of the forest. I tried to plant my feet into the dirt, flailing against his body, but nothing I did worked.

The farther he dragged me into the center of whatever this gathering was, the more eyes were upon me, staring at me with wide eyes and taunting smirks. The smells, the sights, all the sensations of this place were far too real and overwhelming. I wished I had never set foot beyond my house. I should have just stayed home in my misery.

The man heaved me over his shoulder and threw me onto a spot in the ground, back first. I struggled against the pain and lost my breath from hitting the ground so hard. My eyes opened to a crowd of staring faces that had gathered in a circle around me. A circle of stones surrounded a pit of dirt and ash, as if where I was once used to burn something. Or someone. I screamed out at the thought I might be next.

I planted my palms into the dirt and tried to push myself up but was met by some impossible force keeping my limbs bolted to the ground, just like Joe and Nameless did to me. I couldn't believe this was happening again, that I had let myself wander back into this situation.

Someone from the crowd reached in to grab the bottom of my shirt, lifting it up to show my scar to the world. For a second, everyone fell silent except for me.

"What's that symbol doing on her?" someone yelled. "A living *ayidi* with that symbol?"

"She should be dead," another said. She clasped her hands over her face and whimpered.

"How did you get that?" another person asked.

The little blue creature suddenly reappeared, hovering next to my face; a small comfort arrived too late to do much for me. I focused on its tiny blue body as I struggled to lift myself, again finding my body pushing against invisible bonds.

The eyes of the confused crowd transformed into stares of wonder. They made startled noises and started sentences that went unfinished. I couldn't find a way out of this terror.

"It can't be!" someone yelled, pointing toward the creature by my face. "A companion!"

"How can this be?" another shouted.

I saw movement at the edge of the crowd. As the tall, feminine figure stepped forward, the other people rushed to get out of her way, some bowing their heads to her in shame or respect.

"What is this?" she said. A head of blonde hair bobbed above the crowd from where I was lying. No one responded, only moved away as she walked toward where I was in the center of the crowd until she was right beside me; a billowing, kaleidoscopic robe towered over me.

"What have you done?" she asked. Her question was directed toward the crowd. The man who dragged me into this was the first to answer.

"I thought she was an *ayidi*. We were gonna take care of the situation." He bowed his head in shame as he responded.

"Take care of the situation? Can you not see what she is?" the woman said. "She bears the mark. Everything about what you are doing is wrong." The crowd remained silent. She clutched the man by the part of the robe over his chest, shouting something that sounded like a foreign insult before shoving him away. No one bothered to catch him as he tumbled into the ground. The people around him made space for his fall.

"Are you all so quick to forget? It's all too clear that tonight proves that we haven't learned our lesson here after what happened only months ago," she said. "I never want to see an injustice like that again. If anything, *anything*, happens that even comes close, rest assured that your punishment will be far worse than my previous decision. Tonight is supposed to be a gathering of our kind, one of the few times that we can do so in Springfield. Shame on each of you for destroying this most sacred time." Most of the remaining folks who looked at her while she spoke casted their eyes down.

"Come with me," she said. Her hand outstretched. Suddenly, I could move again; my limbs and torso were freed of whatever strange force kept me tacked to the ground. She took my hands into hers and pulled me up, wrapping an arm around my shoulder to steady my trembling body, walking me in a direction away from the crowd. I was scared and confused, but wonderfully still alive.

She gave her parting words to the crowd as we walked away.

"Tonight is over. If I see any of you out here when I return, you too will be punished for this transgression."

No one had the audacity to move while she was still there. I heard a flurry of movement from the crowd. I glanced behind me to see all the strange people shuffling away, except for one stubbornly solitary silhouette who remained firmly in place. The woman beside me turned back around for just a moment, and the two stared at each other. When she yanked her head away, the figure shambled away, muttering something incoherent and shaking their head in discontent.

I should have bolted for the edge of the forest right then. Or better yet, ran as much as I could and not slowed down until I reached my front yard. But I didn't have it in me to make any sudden movements or create a misunderstanding with the person who helped me. Terrified and reeling, I needed a moment of silence to process what happened to me and how I was going to make it out of there without causing another scene.

She walked me to a tent decorated like a festive candy cane and brushed aside the curtain, allowing me to enter first.

"Take a seat," she said as she came in and let the curtain fall back into place behind her. I settled into a pile of cushions. A moment later, the tiny, flying creature joined us and sat on my shoulder. I put my face in my hands, trying to steady my shaking body as flashbacks rippled through my mind. All I had wanted was answers, yet I had found myself so close to being killed a second time. How did I know I was still safe right now? This woman was helpful, but how did I know she didn't mean me harm like everyone had so far? I pulled my hands away from my face, releasing streams of terrified tears. My legs refused to work, and I couldn't get the rest of my body to stop trembling.

The woman stooped down to meet me at eye level. I didn't want to look her in the eye in my current state, wouldn't even be able to see her properly through my blurred vision.

"Hey," she said. "It's alright. Don't be afraid. You're safe with me." She reached into her robe and a folded piece of cloth emerged. She used it to pat down my face and wipe away the moisture from around my eyes until I could finally see her full on for the first time.

She greeted me with a small and welcoming smile. Gazing into her shimmering blue eyes that contrasted with her golden-brown skin, I smiled back. Her wavy hair was almost as blonde as my own and streamed down the sides of her face, collecting in the curls that draped around the shoulders of her robe. She seemed to radiate kindness and competence, but it hit me again that I didn't know this person, still didn't understand what was happening to me, and had no real plans for my escape.

"They were going to kill me!" I said. "If you hadn't come when you did, they would have killed me! But I didn't even do anything. All I wanted was answers! I followed this...this creature and asked it to give me answers. I shouldn't have come here. Why would they do this to me? Why didn't I just stay home?" I was rambling, falling apart in front of the textbook definition of a mysterious stranger. I didn't care anymore. She took my hands into hers.

"I don't know that there is anything I could say to assuage the terror you have experienced. Those people back there were out of line. They are all too tense given the recent occurrences in our community. You did nothing to deserve what just happened. I apologize to you from the bottom of my heart for the unfair mistreatment that you have received." What could I say to that? Why was she apologizing when she was the one to save me?

"I know that you went through something terrible to get that scar. A horror that no one should have to experience. I know that strange phenomena have been happening to you ever since. This creature on your shoulder that follows you without fail. Bizarre incidents that you can't explain. Yet, you were strong enough to survive and to look for answers even though you were afraid."

I squinted my eyes in confusion.

"How do you know that?" I asked.

"I know because you and I are more alike than you know." Her smile grew. The fact this woman already knew so much about what I experienced meant I could either trust her fully, or something mysterious beyond my comprehension was going on. My exhausted mind chose the first option.

"I'm just... I'm tired of being misunderstood. My sister doesn't understand. My parents don't get it. They all just think I'm crazy. But I know I'm not crazy, even though I can't explain the things I've seen. Everything around me right now proves it. I'm sick of being in the dark and confused about everything. I don't want to be afraid anymore."

"You don't have to be," she said. Her voice soothed me like a spoonful of honey. "I know you don't realize it now, but you have the power to do anything you want and more." She was trying to comfort me, but so far, she only added to my confusion.

"What do you mean?" I asked. She pursed her lips and smiled like she was hiding a delicious secret.

"You're like me," she said. "You're made of magic."

"Magic?" I asked in disbelief, my heart racing at the implications. She nodded. A simple word that could explain so much but still left too many unanswered questions. My eyelids fluttered; my lips trembled as I pondered the right questions to ask.

"My name is Alejandra," she said, saving me from my fit of sputtering nonsense. "And yours?"

"Dina," I mumbled.

"Dina, I know that all of this might be hard for you to understand now, but I promise that it will all make sense in time," she said.

"But I'm still so confused. I never wanted any of this."

"It's too late for that now. You're going to have to understand and accept what is happening to you. This change isn't scary. It's beautiful."

"How do you know?" I asked her.

"I know because I went through the same thing. Our stories may have differences, but they are more similar than you can imagine." She grabbed both sides of my face and forced me to look directly into her eyes again.

"Better now?" she asked. I nodded. She smiled and took her hands away.

"I expect that you'll have many questions," she said. "I can give you answers."

"I would like that," I said. She smirked like she had been expecting that answer.

"Excellent. Dina, I would be honored to invite you into my home for the rest of the evening. We have so much to discuss, and our surroundings here won't quite do our conversation justice. I can assure you'll be safer in my home than anywhere else in this city."

My heart yearned for answers, explanations for all I've seen and experienced. If I wanted to rest my head that night, I needed to know I had done all I could to find some sense in this madness. I didn't know who Alejandra was. She could've let the crowd have their way with me and left me to die. But she hadn't. Would it be stupid to take her up on her invitation to her house? Maybe, but not as stupid as returning home empty-handed when I originally set out for answers in the first place.

"Follow me," she said, walking toward the tent's entrance. "And we can be on our way shortly." I got up and followed her out of the tent with the blue creature still clinging to my shoulder with its claws.

I emerged into an empty space. Alejandra's threats were enough to clear the gathering out. The only remnants of the gathering were dark spots in the dirt where the tents had once been propped up and stray bits of cloth and garbage that rolled around in the wind like tumbleweeds. She took a quick look around and a satisfied smile spread across her face before turning back around to face the tent.

She stretched both of her arms out as if preparing to give someone a hug and whispered something unfamiliar. The striped cloth shrank and collapsed in on itself until it was the size of a napkin in the grass. Alejandra bent down to pick it up and stored what remained of the tent in her robe. She then reached out to a spot just beside it in the grass, grabbed something, then stood back up. When she was upright again, I noticed she picked up a long, brown staff that was ornately carved with designs on every inch of the surface. She flipped the staff so that it was parallel to the ground and straddled it with her legs.

"Hop on," she said.

I still didn't move. My eyes were glued to the part of the staff not covered by her body. My body shuddered as another memory returned; Joe and Nameless speeding through the sky on their own staffs, coming toward me again while I was powerless. This was where it happened.

"Dina," someone called out. I shook my head as I returned to the present and heard Alejandra calling my name. Her hand was gently wrapped around my upper arm.

"There is no need to be afraid. I can promise you that you'll never be any place safer."

I hesitated stepping forward, swinging one shaking leg over the staff until I straddled it right behind Alejandra, trying to block the memories bubbling to the front of my mind. Alejandra glanced back at me one last time before we took off.

"I will keep you safe, Dina. Just remember to hold on tight." I wrapped my arms around her waist. The creature's little fingers dug into my shoulder. I took a big gulp of air right before our feet hovered above the ground, then we lifted off into the air. My stomach sank as though I was approaching the top of a rollercoaster.

The wind whipped through my hair, blowing away the memories dying to take up space in my mind of the first time I had ever seen anyone doing what Alejandra and I were doing now. Flying. When I got the courage to peek downward, I saw the city in a way I never witnessed it before, like a set of dollhouses where we were all playthings to a larger being.

Alejandra swooped over a part of the city I don't think I had ever been in. A nicer part of town; the houses were larger than where I lived. She descended just as we were above one of those palatial houses surrounded by a dark fence. We landed in the backyard filled with plants, bushes, and flowers that were colorful enough for me to make out in the night's darkness. I stayed still even after our feet touched the grass, waiting for Alejandra to give me the signal it was safe for me to step away.

When the staff plopped down onto the ground as if it were just an ordinary object, I took the hint it was okay to scoot away from our landing spot. Alejandra leaned down to carry the staff in one of her hands and walked toward the back of her house. She placed her hand on a spot in the wall that was darker than the rest and whispered something I couldn't understand. When she pulled her hand away, the wall separated, creating a new passage into the house. While she stepped forward into her house, and set the staff against a wall, I remained in place, amazed by what I had just seen.

Alejandra turned her head back to face me.

"Come on inside, Dina," she said. "The door won't stay open forever." I came too far to stay outside and remain confused, so I did as she said. When I glanced behind me, the passage disappeared, and the wall looked as if nothing strange happened at all.

I trailed closely behind Alejandra as she led me through one room after the next, destination unknown. Though her home seemed large enough on the outside, the inside seemed endless. Each of the rooms were dimly lit as if she wanted to evoke a sense of calm I couldn't feel while inside of a stranger's house. We passed through rooms of darkly carved furniture, bookcases filled to the brim with titles I didn't get a chance to look at clearly, and bizarre trinkets; strange, abstract pieces of artwork I didn't understand.

A million questions I didn't have the courage to ask buzzed through my mind, so I remained silent, taking everything in and waiting for Alejandra to give me an explanation. Hopefully one that would make sense of everything. I wanted to ask her if she lived alone, whether all this space was devoted to her or if she had a family that was not immediately visible in the rooms we walked through.

As we passed through the rooms, I would sometimes hear banging coming from one of the floors above, perhaps footsteps emanating from some room I couldn't see as if there were someone or something moving in the distance. When she glanced back at me from time to time, I waited for her to comment on the noises, but she didn't acknowledge the sounds. I decided to ignore them as well. Despite Alejandra's kindness, I couldn't fight the feeling I was making a poor decision. It was one of those odd times where things felt right and wrong and I wasn't sure if it was me or my trauma leading my emotions. I had walked into the strange home of a stranger, and into a situation that was becoming more unusual by the minute. But I needed answers, and I didn't want to leave without them.

Our journey ended when we walked into a dimly lit dining room that had a large, dark table in the center, suitable for a banquet, surrounded by several antique-looking chairs. She sat down at the head of the table.

"Have a seat. Anywhere you want," she told me.

I decided quickly to sit down in one of the chairs close to the head of the table. With shaking hands, I pulled the chair out and plopped down into the seat. I craned my neck around to take in the room. The blue creature remained attached to my shoulder.

Alejandra placed both of her hands on the table, closed her eyes, and whispered incomprehensible words. She removed her hands and looked back up at me as a creaking sound emerged from below. I glanced down to see an opening appear in the table. A rippling, putty-like object the color of turquoise sat in the gap in the table, boiling and frothing over.

I jumped as it made a groaning sound like a cough.

"Tea and biscuits for me and our guest," Alejandra commanded, glancing over at me with that sly smile.

The bubbles settled into a blue, glistening surface from which several tentacle-like objects emerged, pulling two mugs, silverware, and a teapot from an unknown source, finishing off with a small tray of cookie-like breads. The tentacles continued to stick out of the surface and writhe around as if searching for something. My eyelids fluttered at the sight in front of me, my body filling with a fearful warmth and my mouth filling with bitter liquid. I fought against the sudden need to flee to a more normal place where things like this didn't exist.

"That will be all," she added. The limbs, or whatever those things were, retreated into the now bubbling surface in the center of the table and disappeared. The putty became solid again and the table closed over it. Everything looked so normal again; I could hardly believe I witnessed another incident I couldn't have imagined but my mind was unable to process properly. *What was that thing? Was it alive, some kind of creature like the one on my shoulder?*

Alejandra picked up the kettle and poured a stream of tea into the cups in front of her.

"It's my newest creation," she said. *Creation?* "Still working out a few minor difficulties, but it gets the job done. I used to have human allies for this kind of help. Guards too. Had to get rid of them all recently. It can be hard to trust anyone around here. Especially with all the madness running around right now. I mostly rely on charms. And some other secrets. Secrets are more trustworthy than people, whose loyalty can be bought or sold so easily."

I nodded my head, too afraid of saying the wrong thing to give a real response. A thump came from somewhere above, but I decided to pass it off.

She leaned forward to hand me one of the full cups. I had no desire to eat or drink anything but didn't want to be rude to the woman showing me hospitality. The cup shook in my hands all the way from the table to my mouth and the hot liquid scalded my throat. I set the cup back down on the table as quickly as I could, almost smashing the glass, spilling tea on my fingers and the table.

"Relax, Dina," she said, placing a hand on my right wrist. "The promise that I made to you before is still the same. Though you have already seen unusual things tonight, none of it can hurt you, especially not while you're in here." She pulled her hand away and reached for her cup to take a sip of her tea. I left my half-spilled mug as is, certain if I tried to drink any more of it, I would spill it everywhere yet again.

"There must be so many things that you want to know,"

Alejandra said. I finally arrived at the place where I could get answers to the questions that troubled me, the incidents that tore my life apart, and yet, I couldn't seem to find the words to express any of them. Where should I begin? Which question would give me the answer to make the most sense? What if her answer threw my mind into further disarray? Part of my tongue went numb from the hot tea, making it that much harder for me to shape any words with my dry mouth.

"I'm not sure how to thank you for saving me tonight," I said, letting the words seep through my lips. I hoped they would lead me to a question that not only made sense but wasn't rude. "I really do appreciate everything, Alejandra. But... who are you?" In the ensuing moment of silence, while my heart pounded in my ears, I hoped I didn't offend her already and cut off my only chance to figure everything out.

She set her tea down, stirring it with a little spoon.

"Of course," she said. "A late introduction is better than none at all. I am Alejandra Enriquez, leader of the community of magic folk who reside in Springfield. But before all of that, most importantly, I am Alejandra Enriquez, a witch."

Witch?

"I have the ability to direct the flow of magic using my mind and body," she continued. "I can see into worlds that ordinary humans, *ayidi*, cannot and have obtained knowledge that most would otherwise regard as mythology or fairy tales."

Witch.

"When I told you before that we share similarities in our stories," she said, "I meant it. You are undergoing a most exquisite metamorphosis. You, like me Dina, are also a witch."

Witch.

I needed water, oxygen, or alcohol. Anything to get rid of the lump in my throat, or the sparks dancing across my mind as if I had just been hit in the head.

"No," I said, shaking my head. "That doesn't...I'm only...it's just that-"

A witch.

This wasn't temporary, or a medical condition I could get rid of. This was a permanent change I didn't ask for, one that I wanted to reverse.

"Dina, I know that you've gone through something traumatic," she said. "And since then, you've seen things that neither you nor anyone else can explain. I don't know if you have tried to share your stories or kept them to yourself, but if you did try to tell anyone, they wouldn't have believed you. Not a single word of it." I waited in silence, every inch of my skin breaking out into a sweat, nausea rapidly rising in my throat.

"You were on the news. The victim of a brutal attack. Left for dead. At the gathering tonight, as soon as everyone saw that symbol on your stomach, they knew exactly who you were. That is a symbol reserved only for specific types of sacrifices." A question that burned inside of me burst from my mouth.

"A *sacrifice*?" I asked. "Why me? What did I do to deserve that?"

"You must understand, what happened to you wasn't your fault," she said. "It was simply a matter of being in the wrong place at the wrong time. All you can do is make good of it, and right now, right before me, I see something amazing."

"This isn't amazing!" I yelled. "What about any of this is amazing? Why did they do this to me?"

"Because they thought that you had seen too much," she said.

"But that wasn't my fault!" I said.

"You're right. None of that was your fault," she said. "You see, we usually disguise the more visible parts of our world with magic to keep ourselves hidden from all of the *ayidi*. But no magic is foolproof. Sometimes a stray human gets sight of our world. If they've only caught a glimpse, we simply let them go. We have different rules, however, if we believe that they have gotten far more than a glimpse." Her words started to touch upon what Joe and Nameless had said to me that night.

"What?" I asked. "Death? Is that your rule for someone who has seen too much?"

"You have to understand, Dina, our world follows different rules from what you may be used to," she said. "We keep our world a secret from everyone else. If an ordinary person has seen too much, we have to kill them. Otherwise, they put all of us at risk for being revealed to everyone. It's happened to us in the past far too many times. Usually to young burgeoning talent not strong enough to protect themselves properly. *Burn the witch.* That is why we have had to create these rules. We are supposed to sacrifice them in a certain way to ensure that their death brings prosperity to our community. That symbol carved into you is a part of that ritual. That's what would have happened to you."

"Then what happened?" I asked. "Why am I still here?"

"The ritual must have gone wrong," she explained. "Your attackers thought they had killed you, but they did not. In certain magical rituals, if a human isn't killed, they will rise again with latent powers activated within them. All that magic going through you... your body and soul will never be the same again. There are two ways to become a witch: you can either be born, or you can be created. Having that kind of power flow through you turned you into the latter. If your attackers had carried out the ritual correctly

"Correctly!" I yelled. "I didn't deserve anything that they did to me. How can you sit here defending them?"

"I am not defending them, Dina, not in the slightest," she said. "What they did to you was unacceptable. They should not have performed the ritual in the first place. You saw something small once, late at night. They should have fled as soon as they realized that you saw them. Even when the circumstances do call for it, the ritual is supposed to be quick and dignified. It's not supposed to involve the kind of torture that they put you through. As the leader of this community, I apologize, from the bottom of my soul, with all my power, for what they did to you. But rest assured, we have taken justice on those two sadistic warlocks. When I found out about their deed, I had them branded and banished. They will never be able to hurt you again."

"After what they did, you only banished them?" I asked.

"Again, the rules are different here, Dina," she said. "Those two warlocks are gone. They wouldn't dare to set foot back into Springfield again without horrific consequences. And you, as excruciating as it is, must move beyond that moment. You can take that horror and turn it into something good."

She paused, stirring her tea with her spoon again, while I struggled to fully comprehend, and pull together, everything she just told me.

"That...that ritual...Changed me? Into a witch?"

Alejandra nodded.

"Exactly," she said. "We call the marvelous little creature that has been by your side a companion. They come from another realm entirely to accompany created witches and warlocks into their initial journey into magic." The creature. My companion. In my mind, the critter transformed from an "it" to a "she." She leapt off my shoulder and onto the plate of biscuits, shoving her face into one and devouring the treat with her previously hidden mouth of sharp teeth.

"I never asked for any of this," I said.

"It doesn't matter whether or not you want it," she said. "I didn't choose this path either. I was born a witch. And despite some of the grief it has caused me, I wouldn't have it any other way. At this stage, you only get to choose whether you embrace it or push it away. Should you decide to reject it, you must remember that you can only bury this so far down. You'll never be able to shield yourself from the other face of this world." I gulped, watching my companion polish off one of the little biscuits before flitting back to my shoulder.

"Reject what you have become and live a life of repression. Or accept everything that you are becoming. Either way, the choice is still yours."

I gazed into my half-full mug of tea, half-expecting to wake up at any moment to find this was all a dream.

"I can tell that you're ready to leave," she said. "Let me give you a ride home. You've experienced too much tonight, and I understand that you will need time to think away from all of this."

A part of me wanted to reject her offer and take a cab, or even walk home instead, anything to pretend my life was still normal and hadn't fallen into a bizarre disarray. When she stood up to make her way to the back entrance, I couldn't help but to follow her through the labyrinth of rooms. We arrived at the wall she made disappear, picking up the staff on her way out.

"Mind telling me where you would like to be dropped off?" she asked. I gave her the name of my general neighborhood before getting on the staff behind her.

We lifted into the sky, passing through the city until the houses below became more familiar. She swooped down in front of a house not too far away from mine. I unmounted the broom with shaky legs.

"Goodbye, Dina," Alejandra said. "I trust we'll be meeting again soon." She gave me one last smile and bowed her head slightly before taking off again, disappearing into the night. I took in a deep breath, then walked into my house, mind in a daze, uncertain of my future.

My life was finally beginning to settle into a strange truth, though not a truth I wanted to accept.

6

—————

"Where were you?" Kayla shouted at me from the living room, where she had been since I had left. My shoulder was empty. The creature must have heard her voice and fled before being seen. "I was about to go out of my mind!" I hardly had the energy to juggle my strange experiences with Kayla's hysterics. Couldn't she just get out of the way?

"I'm sorry, Kayla," I said.

"Where did you go?" she yelled, throwing her arms around her, making the most dramatic gestures possible.

"I didn't know that it was a crime to take a walk outside," I said, ready to end this conversation and return to my bedroom. I stood in the entrance to the living room but made no motions to get any closer to where she stood.

"This wasn't just 'a walk outside', Dina and you know that!" she said. "You haven't left the house in weeks and suddenly you're up walking around in the middle of the night? If you wanted to go somewhere, why didn't you just tell me?"

"I-I don't know," I said. "I don't know what I was thinking. I've been cooped up in here for so long and I just wanted to get out. I didn't mean to scare you, Kayla. I'm so sorry."

"When I woke up and saw that the door was open, I almost called the freaking police!" she said. "Do you have any idea of the kinds of worries that were running through my mind?"

I did, and better than she could've ever imagined or understood. Those very same fears had also trapped me. Only now was I able to overcome them in pursuit of answers. And look where it had gotten me.

"Just- I can't lose you, Dina," she said. She walked up to me and threw her arms around me. I froze beneath her touch, an unusual occurrence in our relationship. Her cheeks were wet with tears.

"We almost already lost you once," she said. "Don't put us through that again."

I wanted to promise my sister she would never have to experience the panicked fear she went through while waiting for me to come home from wherever I had been. But I didn't want to lie. How could I promise she was safe from the same emotional chains I was only beginning to break out of? My mind was still halfway somewhere else, and all I wanted to do was lay down and sort through all that happened to me.

"If you ever need anything, you know that you can ask me, okay?" she said. "Even if it's just a walk around the park. You don't have to go through any of this alone." She spoke as if she knew or understood the isolation that was so heavy it was almost suffocating.

In a moment of weakness, I was tempted to repeat my past mistake and share again the strangeness I witnessed, unloading my burden into someone else's mind.

When she pulled away and looked me in the eye through her tears, I remembered just how terribly that had gone last time. I kept my mouth shut.

"I'm sorry, Kayla," I repeated. "I'm tired."

"Okay," she said. "Go get some rest, Dina. But just remember that I'm here for you, okay?" I nodded and made my way to my bedroom, expecting to find my companion sitting somewhere inside. I closed the door behind me and searched for her but couldn't find her anywhere.

She must have escaped through the open window of another room. If I wanted to see my only other witness to what I saw tonight, I had to wait until the following evening for her to return. Until then, it would just be me and my thoughts, which hopefully wouldn't be enough to send me over the edge.

I tore the spare sheet down from over my mirror, revealing my reflection, more proof of what I experienced. The result of magic? It was the only explanation for everything, but my mind couldn't wrap itself around it, searching for any other reason. My world had been so much smaller, so much less scary, yet carried so little meaning.

In search of materials, I leaned down beneath my bed, which had become a storage space for me. I emerged with an old notebook, the first few pages filled with notes and doodles from a drama class I sat in on for a few days at the local community college. In those days, I had been among other twenty-somethings who spent their days at boring office jobs while dreaming of achieving fame. My days as an aspiring singer, though only months in the past, felt like a lifetime away. In that moment, I would trade about anything to return to that simple time when my biggest worry consisted of wearing the right wardrobe to impress whatever person with connections I met on an ordinary day.

My body pulsed with energy; I was not yet ready to sit. I carried my notebook over to my dresser instead and used it as a standing desk. I scribbled down as much as I could remember. It was the only way I currently had to get these thoughts out of my head and into some other source.

Tonight, I almost died again, I started. What might have happened if Alejandra hadn't come along after I stumbled into their gathering, which I still didn't fully understand? Those people would have killed me right then and there for the "rit-ual" Joe and Nameless tried to perform on me before. Although they didn't seem to enjoy the moment as much as the duo, somehow, they knew who I was. Alejandra knew my story. The scar on my stomach had put a halt in their plans. Despite being a completely ordinary woman not too long ago, I was now marked as one of them, and they recognized that.

Something must have happened in their community after what Joe and Nameless did to me. Had they become more careful after the incident that could have revealed their world to the outside? Maybe that was why they were so eager to get rid of me before Alejandra showed up to put an end to it.

I met the strangest woman who turned out to be my savior.

Alejandra called herself a "leader" of the magical folk in Springfield. Based on how everyone treated her at the gath-ering when she had come to the rescue, this didn't surprise me at all. Those people either respected her or feared her greatly, maybe both. But her title still didn't tell me much. She was a witch too, that much I knew. She could have let the people she led kill me right then and there. She had rescued me and invited me into her home. *Why?* Was it out of a sense of respon-sibility since two of her people screwed up and left me alive? Or was it something else? Could I trust her? Right about now, she seemed like the only person in this new world I could trust.

Her home was out of this world.

Since I was back in my house, Alejandra's home felt like something out of a dream, an oddity that didn't belong in my reality. What were the strange noises I could have sworn I heard as we had walked through her house that Alejandra didn't seem to notice, especially the ones that sounded like footsteps? Maybe they were everyday occurrences in her large, creaky house she learned to ignore. I had no idea whether she lived alone, or if her house could hold more strangeness like the table she commanded to serve us.

The thought of those tentacles reaching out from a mass in the center of the table, responding to speech and muttering its own simple sentence, made me shudder. Had that...thing... been alive? She referred to it as her "creation". Did she have others like that lying around her house too? I didn't remember her referring to anyone else she lived with, but that didn't mean anything if she was trying to ease me into all of this. I was having a hard enough time accepting her words as it was.

She gave me some answers. But I still have so many questions.

If she was right, that I had now become a...a "witch" as she had called it – what did that mean? I could use...magic? I scribbled "witch" and "magic" down onto the paper below but still found little relief. They still sounded like words out of a storybook, out of some play I would have read back when I cared about my dramatic career, but not terms that could explain what was happening to me.

New images flashed before my eyes of Alejandra drying my tears as we talked in the privacy of the tent. Flying through the night and seeing the city from a new perspective.

I was grateful for those memories for holding at bay the painful remembrances of the night that had changed everything, though eventually those returned. It was time for me to give up my game of detective for the night. My notebook went back under my bed. When I laid down to go to sleep, I saw the sun peeking out just over the horizon through my window.

I pulled the covers over my head, not sleepy yet, but needing some way to reset and return to my own reality where things like magic and witches didn't exist.

7

It should have been my decision whether I wanted to deal with this fantasy world of magic or not. What if all I wanted to do for the rest of my days was remain beneath the sheets, hiding away from the reality of what's going on outside? I wasn't a part of that world anyway. Everyone else was getting on with their lives. The sun rose and set as if nothing changed, as if my life hadn't been flipped upside down and had all the senses and patterns shaken out of it. I could give up trying, completely stopping my search for answers which hadn't been satisfying anyway. Should I keep going down that rabbit hole? Or would it make more sense for me to stay where I was? Wandering outside only led me to encounter another close brush with death. What Alejandra told me still seemed impossible. I wanted to return to the simple way my life was before all of this happened. I didn't want these changes that were forced upon me to be permanent.

When my companion returned the night after the carnival, I tried to ignore her. I shooed her away as she tried to settle onto my arm again, asking her to leave me be while I stared at the ceiling. Instead of leaving, she sat on the dresser across from my bed for hours, facing me, somehow staring at me without eyes. She was gone by the time I woke up after the sun rose. She appeared at my window again the following night, hovering outside as if waiting for my permission to enter. This time, I closed the window so she couldn't get inside. I adjusted my position with my back facing her. When I looked back over sometime later, she was gone.

I jolted awake from a dream one evening, the kind of dream where you can't remember specifics but only the emotion. All I could feel was falling and suffocating beneath some force. My dream had no color or visuals. When my eyes popped open, I took in deep gulps of air; my skin was covered with a sheen of sweat. I scooted to the edge of my bed, shaking my head at the fact that even my sleep wasn't peaceful. My room felt stifling hot. I got on my feet and walked over to the window to open it, only to find it had already been opened. My companion was sitting on the windowsill, somehow able to squeeze through that small space into my room.

"How did you get in here?" I asked, as if she was capable of speaking. Her eyeless face, with only a thin line for a mouth, turned to "look" at me. *Why had she returned?* She was like the pet I never asked for. Look at the trouble she had gotten me into last time I asked her to show me some answers. I managed to avoid any weirdness so far since she had been gone. If I could shoo her away for good, I could distance myself from this craziness and get a move on to something else if I could muster up the strength.

"Why did you come back? Find someone else to help. I don't want anything else that you have to show me." I got no response from her whatsoever, not even a change in her movements. What could I do to get her to go away? Would I have to hurt her? Make her feel as afraid as I always felt? Clearly, only trying to ignore her wasn't doing the trick. I didn't want to bring her any harm, but I wasn't sure I had any other option.

"Why don't you just leave?" I asked, my eyes pooling with moisture. I fanned my hands at her, trying to shoo her away. "Get out of here!" Her wings began to move back and forth, and she hovered above the windowsill. For a moment, I thought she was going to leave, for good.

Something in the room changed.

The back of my neck prickled as if someone was in the room with me. A moment later, my suspicions were confirmed when I heard a knock coming from the wall to my right. Someone, or something, was trying to get in.

My companion flew into the air, dashing in random directions in a frenzy. She opened her mouth to reveal her teeth again and made a strange clicking sound, as if she too could sense something wasn't right.

I didn't want to turn around, but as the light knocks turned into loud banging, I found I had little choice. I slowly twisted my head around, followed by the rest of my body, to face the source of the sound. The mirror's glass moved on its own, rattling like something was forcing its way out.

Forcing the tensed muscles in my legs to move, I took a step toward the mirror, fighting against the paralysis that would have kept me staring instead of doing anything. My companion appeared in the corner of my vision, flitting back and forth in front of the mirror.

I stood squarely in front of the mirror, watching my reflection shift slightly as the mirror continued to move. The crack I made previously in the glass, fractured the top of my head in my reflection. All I could see was my likeness in the glass, without any indication of what might be causing the sound and movement.

My heart leapt into my throat when my reflection changed before me. My blue eyes shifted to a dark red. I jumped back away from the mirror, but that wasn't the only change to come.

My pale skin darkened before my eyes, becoming black as a

shadow, and my corrupted reflection moved on its own. Its mouth opened, displaying rows of shark-like teeth, and it lifted an arm to point at me with a black claw. The tip of its talon emerged from the glass, followed by the rest of its hand, as this hallucination became real. I stumbled backward, tripped on the edge of my bed, and fell. My back slumped against the mattress. A full arm emerged from the glass straight toward me.

I tried to ignore this world; I wanted to return to a place where everything made sense, but even when I tried to stay away from it, it still found me. This could be it. The end of all my efforts; the conclusion to a tragic story all brought about by factors beyond my control.

I was trembling, stuck in place, useless as a second arm emerged parallel to the first. This thing entered my world, eyes glowing like fire. It was as if this creature was made of pure fear. Things like this couldn't exist, weren't meant to exist in my old life. How was I supposed to handle this now? What was I supposed to do to protect myself if all I wanted was to live a semi-normal life again?

A leg stuck out, and I still didn't know what to do beyond shaking on the floor. I wanted to put my head into my hands and cover my face until this was all over.

My companion flew in front of my face, distracting me from the horror in my mirror. She grabbed one of my arms with both hands, and then the other. I didn't know what she wanted me to do beyond lift them up, so I did just that, palms pointed toward the mirror, where a second leg became visible.

"What do I do?" I asked her. "Tell me what I'm supposed to do!"

She opened her mouth and clicked. That was her attempt to tell me some important information that could save my life, but it didn't help me at all. She flew away and settled on my shoulder so the only thing I could see in my view was the being in the mirror. Every part of me wanted to run out the door, but would I find safety anywhere else? Would this thing follow me until it got me?

All its limbs, and part of its face, were out of the mirror, while his chest remained submerged in the glass. The thing was all the way out when something clicked inside my head.

I was tired of being afraid, sick of cowering away from life because of what had happened to me. Damn this creature. Damn Joe and Nameless and all the other witches and warlocks, and whatever in this strange world that tried to take away my life and left me an empty shell of who I had used to be.

The creature stepped onto the carpet with one of its claws, creating smoke where it stood. It was so close; I could feel its heat on my skin. Perhaps it was close enough to kill me.

I screamed.

The palms of my hands went tingly, and it felt like something was being pulled out of them. An invisible force flew out against the mirror, shattering it into tiny pieces that flew everywhere. My arms flew up against my face to protect myself from the blast.

My breathing was shallow, and I was too shaken to drop my arms. I peeked at the space between my arms. I saw an empty mirror frame surrounded by shattered glass, some of which had implanted into my skin though I felt no pain. The paint and material in the wall behind the frame were chipped and damaged. The creature was gone. The only evidence it was here was the dark footprint it left on my carpet in front of me.

My shaking arms dropped slowly to my side. I pushed myself up, staring at the damage I caused, confused by what happened. I reached up to touch my companion with one of my hands. She grabbed my index finger with both of hers.

My head was pounding. I opened my mouth to release all that had built up within me from this incident. But then I heard a scream that wasn't my own.

I turned around to find my bedroom door open and Kayla standing in the middle of it, eyes and mouth wider than I've ever seen them. I wasn't sure how long she was standing there, but I knew it was long enough for her to witness things she shouldn't have that might change her life as much as it transformed mine.

        8
    ———————

Kayla sat across from me in the kitchen. I could barely meet her eyes. We both sat in silence, as if we were waiting for the other one to make the first move. Kayla stared down at the table, shaking her head.

"We've gotta get you to a hospital," she said. "You've got glass and cuts all over you."

I glanced down at my arms, fully aware of the cuts and pieces of glass that broke into my skin, yet hardly any pain registered. How had I gotten into the kitchen in the first place? The last solid thing I remembered was sitting shocked in front of the broken mirror and looking over at my sister as she came toward me to help me to my feet. I was so light-headed and out of it. My companion was gone, probably flew away shortly after Kayla discovered me. After what just happened to me, my physical injuries were the least of my worries.

"Kayla, what did you see?" I asked. She stood up and pushed her chair in, walking over to the sink to pour herself a glass of water.

"I saw you sitting in front of your bed with the mirror

broken right in front of you," she said. "How did you even break the mirror, Dina? Why would you even do that?"

Based on how pale her face was, I knew she wasn't telling the truth. I still didn't know how long she was standing in the doorway, but she surely must have seen more than she was letting on. My companion on my shoulder. The mirror shattering on its own. The burnt spot in the carpet where that demonic being set foot into my room. I had another witness in my life to the impossible, proof it was real.

"Really, Kayla?" I asked. "You didn't see anything else?"

"What the hell even happened to you?" she asked. She took a sip of her water, looking down into her glass and not at me.

"What do you mean what happened to me?" I asked. "Something was trying to get into my room through the mirror."

"What? Like a break in? Was someone trying to break in through your room?" I couldn't believe she was acting this dense. Was she so much in denial she wouldn't admit to seeing what was right in front of her face? I was right back to where I had been after being released from the hospital trying to explain myself to Kayla, only to have her pass me off as crazy.

"I know you saw something, Kayla!" I said. "Tell me what you saw! Something tried to enter my room through the mirror and almost killed me! I had to defend myself by breaking the mirror! Tell me that you saw it too! I know you did."

"I don't know what you're talking about, Dina," she said. Her arm was shaking so hard, some of the water sloshed over the side of the glass. "But we need to get you some help."

Kayla had the luxury of trying to convince herself what she saw wasn't real, trying to pass it off with some logical explanation that made even less sense than what happened. I had no chance of doing the same when I had almost died. I realized no matter how long I sat there, trying to pry an answer out of her, I wasn't going to get the truth. It was too easy for her to write me off as a traumatized, hallucinating victim than to admit she saw something terrifying and inexplicable.

I wasn't safe outside. I wasn't safe in my home with Kayla. I wasn't even safe in my room. I had only one option left, one last place where I might be understood and secure.

When Kayla went to bed, I stayed up all night in the living room, staring at the TV with the volume all the way down. I didn't want to set foot into my room again with all the debris still laying around. It was too much of a reminder I was powerless to stop any of that from happening again.

My eyes glazed over as the hours went by. I fell into a fog somewhere between sleep and wakefulness. Whenever Kayla passed by throughout the next day asking questions, usually something about going to the hospital, I just nodded and grunted. I was slightly aware of the throbbing pain in my arms and the nicks of blood on my clothes, but hardly cared enough to do anything about it. Instead, I waited until the sun fell. My only anchor in this world returned, emerging into my sight from some opening in the house, fluttering in front of me like she knew I was expecting her.

I was sick of being powerless, letting the universe throw whatever it wanted at me, only for me to retreat further into myself, into a place of terror where I was too fearful and confused. The memory of what Alejandra told me about how I could keep trying to push magic away from my life, but I wouldn't be successful, returned to the front of my mind.

When my blue companion settled onto the top of my hand, I felt like my decision was made for me. "Do you remember how to get to Alejandra's?" I asked her. She nodded her head in delight.

9

I couldn't believe I was sitting in Alejandra's dining room again. Of my experiences, my uncertainty, my fear of potentially putting myself in danger again, I found myself sitting in the same seat from my first visit. My mind still wild with questions.

I couldn't remember the walk over or how my companion led me to my destination. I couldn't recall leaving my house or even putting shoes on in preparation for the journey. It was like I asked for my companion's directions one moment, and the next we were coming up on a familiar place from a different angle.

My vision was blurry, mind foggy, with only one thought guiding me forward: finding safety at Alejandra's again. I almost didn't recognize Alejandra's house from the front. When my companion stormed toward the front door, I chased after her, banging on the front door.

"Alejandra!" I yelled. "Alejandra, it's me! It's Dina! Let me in!"

After her previous offer, I hoped she was still willing to grant me a second chance to enter her home and stay a little longer this time. I didn't stop banging, calling out for her, and repeating my name until I heard footsteps approaching the door. The person on the other side pulled a slide open, revealing completely white eyes surrounded by blue skin through a slit in the door. This wasn't Alejandra. Who was this? Some strange being that also took refuge in her home? I couldn't let the rising, sickening fear get to me. I needed to find Alejandra again at all costs.

"I'm Dina!" I yelled. "I'm looking for Alejandra! Please let me in! Let me in!" There was another sliding sound before the slit disappeared. I heard more footsteps going off in the opposite direction.

The sounds on the other side of the door fell silent. I didn't know what that thing was that greeted me, but I knew this was a terrible idea. Alejandra wasn't going to save me. I was all on my own. Now down on my knees, I kept banging on the door with the palms of my hands, calling out for Alejandra again in the silence.

After what felt like an eternity, I heard more footsteps, but with a different pattern approaching the door. I remained poised with my ear against the door, waiting for the signal to give me either good or bad news as to the identity of the person on the other side of the door.

The door opened. When I looked up into her face, I fell into her arms. She knelt to catch me. I didn't have time to ask or even wonder to myself about what answered the door that obviously wasn't Alejandra. My mouth dropped open and I unleashed a tale about everything I experienced since I met her, especially the creature trying to attack me from my mirror. She placed a finger on my lips and shushed me.

"All in due time, Dina," she said. "Take a deep breath. This is your new home now if you would like it to be."

Alejandra sat in silence, listening to every word I had to say. We sat across from each other, resting on pillows in one of the many decorated rooms in her house. My companion was nestled in a smaller pillow beside me. She watched me intently, nodding from time to time. Her face said it all for me.

I believe you.

When I came to the end, Alejandra grasped both of my wrists, looking over my injuries from the shattered glass.

"Hold them still," she said as she let go. She rose from her seat to pull down a small carved wooden case from one of the many shelves and set it down on the floor next to her. I thought I could hear more sounds in the distance, maybe footsteps. Perhaps it had been that blue thing that answered the door walking around. I wanted to ask her whether there was anyone else here with us, but it wasn't my place to demand answers when Alejandra had invited me into her home for a second time.

She stuck her hand inside the box. Her hand emerged with a container of something green, sparkling like an emerald, that she uncorked. She spread the paste into the palm of one of her hands and rubbed her hands together. She placed a hand on my arms, closing her eyes and spreading the paste all over both sides, chanting. As her hands passed over areas where the paste had already been placed, the material hardened, forming a cast-like layer over my arms. I felt my breathing and my heart slow down. When she took her hands away, the material shrunk until it felt like the blood pressure monitor nurses used, before shattering into pieces on the floor. My arms emerged with smoother, shinier skin. The bits of glass were now gone, and the cuts shrank to small scabs.

"This won't make your wounds disappear entirely, but it will make the healing process that much faster," she said.

"Th-thank you, Alejandra," I said, turning my arms back and forth, looking for an imperfection I could not find.

Instead of interrupting me, or giving a look of disbelief like Kayla, she kept both of her hands covered on mine. She nodded her head from time to time, looking down and shaking her head as if she knew exactly what I was talking about. When I was done letting the words spill out of my mouth, I looked down and shook my head back and forth in disbelief. I finally gave someone the full story of what really happened to me within the past week.

I waited for Alejandra to pick up where I left off, to give me an answer even if it was one I didn't want to hear.

"I know you still must be shaken up by your experience," she began. "But I am proud of you for handling that creature as you did. From what you're describing, that sounds like a *metluk*, not particularly the most powerful, but terrifying all the same. Relatively harmless compared to a lot of others of its kind. You see, there are creatures"

"Harmless?" I said. "*Harmless?* That thing left a burn mark on my carpet. Its arms and legs were coming out of the mirror. It was headed right toward me!"

"I know that was frightening," Alejandra said. "As you will learn as a witch, there are plenty of creatures that live beyond our physical realm of experience. Sometimes some of them try to break into ours, not all of them with the best intentions, although they can't always understand that. This creature was probably attracted to the appearance of new magic and sought some of that energy and power for itself. Regular witches can encounter them from time to time over the years. Repelled by the proper spells and charms, and treating the mirrors in your house, you can repel them and protect yourself. I can teach you how to do that and much more."

"I don't even care what that thing was," I said. "I just never want to feel this way again. It came into my room and almost killed me. Even my sister saw it, but she won't admit it. I know she did. She's trying to spin it all into a different story, but she can't deny that she saw something bizarre! She knows that I'm not making this all up!"

"It can be difficult for ordinary folks to accept the presence of magic in the world," Alejandra said. "Think of yourself. You were only introduced to the idea recently, and in a most terrifying way. Yet, you're already making strides from where you once were. The way that your sister leads her life does not make it necessary for her to even begin to ponder the existence of the paranormal. It would be far easier for her to deny what has happened to you, blaming it all on the trauma caused by something far more mundane, and even for her to deny what she herself saw when that being tried to enter your room. She doesn't have the same pressures that have been placed on you and that have been guiding your life ever since."

No matter how hard I tried, I couldn't think of a response that would match what Alejandra expressed. I knew she was right, but I couldn't stop myself from feeling the hurt at not being believed. Yet again mistaken for *crazy*, whatever that word meant. It was the world that had gone crazy. Or maybe the world been crazy all along, and I just hadn't known it yet.

"All I know is that every day I wake up and I don't know what's going on," I said. "I don't know why anything is happening to me. I can't handle feeling like this anymore. I don't want to feel so afraid. So powerless. I'm stuck and I can't find my way out."

"You no longer need to be afraid," she said, gently grabbing my hand.

"You have great power within you. You just haven't learned how to use it yet. Teaching you how to defend yourself against creatures like the *metluk,* that are more of a nuisance in the grand scheme of this world than anything truly dangerous, would only be the first step. So much more lies ahead for you, Dina."

She rubbed my hand with her thumb, shaping the corner of her mouth into a small smile. Again, I thought I could hear those noises coming from somewhere in the house but ignored them. Here, Alejandra was talking to me about magic, the kind of power that could transform my life forever. I no longer had the energy to keep pushing it away. The only other option I had was to lie hopelessly in bed, waiting for whatever else this universe had to throw at me.

"I can help you, Dina," she said. "If you are ready."

What would even be the point in trying to return to my old life? I had nothing waiting for me there except cards of false sympathy from people who looked at me with pity. A "career" as a singer I always knew was never going to take off. A stupid office job I hadn't gone back to since the attack and didn't care to return to, anyway. Even if I tried to stay away, this new world I had discovered wouldn't leave me alone.

"I can't go back, Alejandra," I said. "It's too late for my old life. I think that I'm ready to begin."

"You think?" Alejandra asked.

"No," I said. "I know that I'm ready to start."

"Very well," she said. She gathered up the parts of her robe that brushed the floor as she stood and walked toward the door.

"Before we can get started, we need you to be in a better place mentally. You need to rest. We'll always have tomorrow." She held out a hand to help me stand up. My companion flew back onto my shoulder.

I trailed closely behind Alejandra as she led me through the hallway. The noises I thought I'd heard became so faint. I considered I exaggerated them, or they were the ordinary sounds of a house.

Alejandra led me to a door at the top of a large staircase. She turned the knob zend pushed the door open before standing aside, holding out an arm toward the room to encourage me to enter. I stepped inside of a bedroom as large as the one I had back home but decorated far better. The room had a four-poster bed, complete with layers of fluffy pillows and sheets and surrounded on both sides by its own curtains.

An opened door on the right-hand side of the room held a private bathroom. I wondered about when the last time this bedroom had been used, or whether it was still someone else's that she was temporarily using to house me, her guest.

"Make yourself at home," she said.

"Alejandra, thank-" I said, turning around, only to find that she was already gone.

My companion left my shoulder and flitted down onto a pillow at the head of the bed. I took my shoes off and slipped beneath the topmost blanket, clutching the fringes on the end.

My moment of solitary silence since I had gotten here allowed my mind to roam freely. A queasiness sat in the pit of my stomach which no amount of adjusting would relieve. I tossed and turned while my doubts crept back up to the surface.

You're a stranger to her. And you're in her house.

Those sounds? What if they're dangerous?

She's a stranger to you.

What really was that thing *that let you in?*

You're still so lost.

You don't really know anything.

No, I thought. *This is the way forward.* I wanted to trust in Alejandra and everything she offered. She was the only one who could give my experiences meaning. She was the only one who had tried to help. All that doubt was just fear from my past trying to chain me down.

I fought my doubt with warm, recent memories of our interactions, my only source of hope these past few months.

She rescued you at that gathering.

She listened to you when no one else would.

She has the answers that no one else can provide.

You may be strangers now.

But it doesn't need to stay that way.

She has the answers.

She's the only one who cares.

My arms and legs loosened, soothed as I relived her moments of kindness. I couldn't deny there were a lot of unknowns, even with Alejandra herself. But she had proven herself trustworthy enough to me. She was my only support in a world that transformed before my eyes.

Even in a bed that wasn't my own, the need to sleep overtook me quicker than it usually did. My eyelids closed against my will as I nestled into the mattress. Before my great journey to the world of peace sleep provided me, I put my trust in Alejandra's words, letting the warmth squash the stubborn uncertainty fluttering at the back of my mind.

10

My eyes opened the next morning to a room that wasn't my own. The dark red walls looked and felt foreign. I clenched my fists and darted my eyes from one part of the room to the next, letting my memories slowly catch up to me. Once I was caught up, I pushed myself up in bed, planted my forehead in one of my hands, and shook my head. What felt like another close encounter with death was, according to what Alejandra told me, little more than a creature meant to cause mischief that wouldn't be able to do me much harm. I had been so certain last night, still shaking off the experience Kayla had tried to deny.

I heard footsteps approaching the bedroom, followed by a knock at the door.

"Breakfast," someone on the other side said. "Downstairs."

The unrecognizable voice was far too deep and masculine to belong to Alejandra. So maybe she wasn't alone in this house. I waited another moment to see if they would open the door to reveal themselves, but soon heard their footsteps growing more distant. Whoever they were, I wouldn't get the chance to look at them just yet.

The doubts crept back up, going through the arguments from the previous night. What was I doing here? Something was still pulling me back home, discouraging me from trying to continue this stupid quest that would only get me killed for good this time. What was I thinking trying to join the world of magic? With the help of someone I barely know? The thought made me feel stupid. I tried to shake off the thoughts and fill myself with the same warmth I had conjured the evening before. No matter how uncertain, unrealistic, or even ridiculous the path Alejandra was laying out for me seemed, it was the only option forward I had. Coming all this way to just wimp out and return to a house that was no longer my home was not an option.

I ran my hands through my hair and got out of bed. My companion fluttered close beside me, still the only constant in my life. After slipping my shoes back on I opened the door to enter the hallway, finding everything silent. The hallway was stretched out to my left, filled with closed doors that held unknown treasures or dangers. This was no time for curiosity. I turned back toward the staircase and walked downstairs, retracing my path to the dining room that was my most visited spot in Alejandra's home so far.

"Good morning, Dina," Alejandra said. She sat at the head of the table. This morning, she wore a less elaborate robe than the previous ones I'd seen.

"How did you sleep?" she asked with a smile.

"Good," I said, glancing down at the spread laid out on the table. My mouth watered instantly. I hadn't realized I was hungry until the tempting scent of a freshly cooked meal wandered into my nostrils.

"Feel free to help yourself," she said. "I already ate." The plate in front of her held only remnants from the meal she had already eaten. I took a seat at the side of the table that was close to her and grabbed an empty plate. My hands reached out on their own and snatched pastries, followed by sausages and biscuits with gravy. I didn't want to be rude or anything, but I couldn't wait to dig in. Before I devoured my food, I placed a pastry on the table next to me for my companion's morning meal.

I was only midway through eating when I wondered how the food had gotten there in the first place. Had Alejandra risen early and cooked this all herself? Or was it another member of her household I hadn't met yet? It could have been the blue "person" that initially greeted me at the front door the night before, or whoever had knocked on my door this morning. Besides that, there was so much food set out at the table it made me think this breakfast wasn't just for us.

"How are you feeling this morning?" Alejandra asked. "Refreshed?" I dropped the sausage I was eating back onto my plate and looked back up at her.

"Yes," I said. "I really don't know how to thank you for letting me in here and giving me a place to sleep last night. And for all of this." I gestured toward the food around us. Her smile grew.

"It is my pleasure to help those who need it," she said. "And you, Dina, have quite the road ahead of you, now that you have decided that this is the path that you want to lead."

The insecurities from this morning crept back up again, taking on the voices of Kayla and our parents telling me that I was unwell and needed to go "see someone". That was their polite way of saying they wanted this blemish in their lives to disappear. Again, I reminded myself this was the only way forward and turning back was not an option.

"You haven't changed your mind, have you?" she asked after I hesitated.

"No, of course not, Alejandra," I said. "Not at all. Just some uncertainties, is all."

"I can tell you this much, Dina, no matter what decisions

you make, there will always be an element of uncertainty. I've been on this earth for many years now, practicing my craft and traveling to improve my abilities when I can. Even now I sometimes feel afraid. Memories from my childhood like to stand in the way and remind me of those times when I was nothing but a freak and an outcast. And you know what I do? I remind myself that I have lived an amazing life, have had experiences that ordinary folks can only dream about, and every day I wake up excited to continue. Taking on a student such as yourself is a part of my journey, too. It's hard to tell what the future holds for us, but I know that this experience can only enrich us, no matter how hard it gets."

A million questions about Alejandra bubbled up behind my closed lips. She still looked young, maybe in her late thirties. Yet, the way she spoke and the experiences she alluded to gave the impression she was much older. Maybe she was older, and magic was to blame? And if she had been a "freak" too, how did she found her own path? She told me before she was born a witch. Had she also found her own teacher? A previous version of the experience we were about to have? Was she from Springfield? How long had she been here? Would I be the only student she ever taught?

"Do you have something that you would like to ask?" she asked me. I tightened my lips and shook my head. I was unsure whether any of my questions were appropriate or if I could word any of them in a way that didn't sound like I was being rude and throwing her kindness and hospitality right back in her face.

"Well, if you do," she said, rising from her seat. "Hold onto them in the back of your mind. We'll have much time to discuss whatever you want later today." Her attention shifted from me to the door, which my back was facing. As she walked to the dining room's door, I craned my neck around to see what she was looking at.

Once I caught sight of the person, I could not stop myself from staring. The person's presence had answered my question about whether Alejandra lived alone. For all I know, they could have been the source of the sounds I've been hearing.

"Dina," Alejandra said with her arm wrapped around the young woman at her side.

"This is my daughter, Lisa. Lisa, this is the lovely woman I was telling you about who will be staying with us for a while." Lisa was Alejandra's younger reflection: same sharp blue eyes, deep brown- golden skin, blonde hair. But Lisa's hair was cut shorter, the curls stopping at her shoulders, and her ordinary pants and shirt around her narrower frame contrasted with the colorful robs Alejandra always wore.

When Alejandra walked into the gathering of witches and warlocks, it was easy to tell why they all stopped to listen and pay their respects without knowing a single thing about their world. Lisa carried herself with an air of uncertainty, fidgeting and looking at the floor. *How old is she?* Her youthful appearance gave no real answers. *Is she a teenager? College-aged? An early twenty-something just a few years younger than me? How old is Alejandra?*

Lisa made eye contact with me for only a fleeting moment before casting her eyes back down. The way she hopped from one foot to the other made me think she wanted to leave as soon as possible, like she had been interrupted in the middle of whatever she had been doing to come down here.

Her lips moved a little, but I couldn't hear anything.

"Hi Lisa! It's...nice to meet you." No response. I couldn't understand why she reacted to me like that. Was this ordinary teenage angst, if she was indeed a teenager, or was she simply uncomfortable having a new person staying in her house?

"Aren't you going to speak to our guest?" Alejandra asked her. Lisa stared down at her shuffling feet.

"Hi," she said. I didn't think I would get much more from her than that.

"Don't you want some breakfast?" Alejandra asked.

"I'm not hungry," Lisa said.

"Very well. You may be dismissed."

Lisa didn't wait for Alejandra to remove her arm before she turned around and stomped down the hallway, slamming a door somewhere in the house. Alejandra returned to her seat and sighed.

"Teenagers. She won't bother trying to involve herself in the outside world, so I teach her here. She's practically afraid to leave the house. Surely you must understand that." I nodded my head only out of a subtle fear of what would happen if I didn't.

"As I've mentioned to you before, she's far safer in here than anywhere outside. Especially with my position. I can't imagine any harm coming to my daughter because some witch or warlock with a grudge wants to get back at me for some misperceived slight. At least here I can protect her. Just like I can protect you."

How was it that Alejandra hadn't mentioned her daughter to me before now? I went back through our past conversations, trying to see if I missed her telling me about Lisa. Had I just been too preoccupied with what was going on in my life and the decisions I needed to make about my future to really listen to what Alejandra had to say about her own?

"As long as magic is your priority, you will always have a home here."

"Thank you, Alejandra," I said, feeling like I couldn't say that phrase or express my gratitude to her enough.

"Now that you have rested and eaten, are you ready to make your decision?" Despite the uncertainties that wanted to drag me back down before and crawl my way back to my old house, I felt like my decision was already made. I looked Alejandra straight in the eye before I responded.

"Yes," I said to her. "I'm sure."

"If you are serious, the tradition is 30 days and 30 nights of study before you can be initiated into my coven. It would be best for you to remain in my home throughout this time." Somehow the idea of staying in Alejandra's house for a month scared me less than going back into the outside where I would be vulnerable.

"I will go through everything with you, step by step," she said. "But you must know that there is no turning back from this."

"I understand," I said. She took my hand into hers.

"You must have friends, family. Is there anyone you would like me to send a message to?" she asked.

"Yes," I answered. "Only one person."

AFTER GIVING ME PAPER, a pen, and an envelope, Alejandra left me in the dining room to write a brief letter.

Dear Kayla,

~~Hello~~

~~I hope~~

~~How~~

Do not worry about me. I am in a much better place now. I know I left in such a hurry, but there was no time to say goodbye. I will see you as soon as I can. Send mom and dad my regards.

~~Since~~

~~Best~~

With Love,

Dina

I set the pen down, still unsure if I had written what I really wanted to say. I forced myself to get up from the table and let Alejandra know I was done. She promised it would be delivered promptly. The letter was another step to distance myself from the unremarkable life I had once lived.

11

———

No matter how much my negative thoughts tried to pull me away, it was too late to turn back now. Even now, the words were still spinning around my mind as Alejandra and I descended the staircase in increasing darkness with one of Alejandra's hands holding and guiding mine. Her robe, a simple, pattern-less deep purple, billowed around her with each step.

Alejandra had gone through the ritual with me step-by-step. What to say. What to expect. When I walked down the staircase behind her, clad in my own simple robe of green with my companion clinging to my right shoulder, my stomach tightened and a bitterness filled my mouth. I felt like I was about to throw up. I wasn't ready for this. I needed more time, another round of preparation to instill some confidence in me before I made this journey. What was I thinking? This was madness.

Alejandra stopped suddenly, even though we hadn't reached the bottom of the staircase. I came to a stop as well.

"Remember what we promised," she said.

Alejandra and I had washed ourselves in a small pool of

specially treated water that she kept in another room of her house. I repeated each line after her to the best of my ability. My tongue felt clumsy, but I managed. We ducked our open hands into the water and rubbed it over our bodies. The ritual hadn't officially started, but I was already feeling the flutters and jitters of anticipation for what was to come. As I prepared, my mind ran through all that Alejandra had told me. She cast an appraising glance and seemed to sense my growing apprehension. She grabbed both of my arms and told me, "I will soon be your instructor. No matter what happens, while we are performing this rite so that you can begin your journey of becoming a witch, I promise that I will let no harm come to you. You have to believe that, Dina."

I took in another deep breath, pulling me back into the present.

"I remember," I said. "I'm ready."

Alejandra turned back around and continued our descent into another part of her house I'd never seen before. We soon came to the bottom of the staircase, and I felt like despite Alejandra's best efforts to help me through this, nothing could prepare me for the adventure that was soon to come.

The basement was lit with the barest bit of light given off by candles that were set in the floor, forming a part of the intricate carved design sprawled out across the entirety of the basement's floor. I tried to trace the shapes with my eyes, unable to understand how all the patterns fit together. I thought back to something Alejandra said shortly after we finished cleansing ourselves.

"On your journey, you will see and feel the impossible. You will be terrified at times, that much is guaranteed. But you will gain power and knowledge. Your life will never be the same. Whatever happens, focus on my eyes."

Her eyes caught mine as she guided me to the center of the floor. In the flickering of the candlelight, I barely made out her sharp blue irises. She promised to protect me and so far, kept her word. My fight against the negativity trying to take over my moment continued, and I struggled to regain my confidence and trust in what I was doing. I longed to return to the moment we rinsed ourselves in the cool water, the goal ahead of us clear, with hardly anything concrete to frighten me. I tried to trudge that up momentarily, and the fleeting calm, to get me through this.

Alejandra sat cross-legged in the middle in one of the sub-circles in the floor's design. I sat in the sub-circle across from her and mimicked her posture; my companion was resting in my lap.

"You're getting scared," Alejandra said as though she could smell my fear. I could not look away from her gaze.

"Remember what I said before." She then held out her arms to me. I reached out my hands to clasp hers. This momentous undertaking would spark the true separation between who I had once been and the person I wanted to become.

"Think about why you have decided to become a witch," Alejandra said. "Think about the circumstances that have brought you to this point in your life."

I allowed that fatal scene to play out before me, feeling the powerlessness all over again. All those times I laid in bed one day after another, feeling too horrible to do anything else, played out in my mind. I recalled my encounters with the para-normal, crashing that gathering and having an entity enter my home, events that could have become disastrous for me. Each memory unleashed a little bit of my frustration, culminating in a final relieving scream.

Alejandra said my name before rattling off phrases in the language of magic. I remembered their meaning from our previous run through:

"You agree to undertake this journey to become a witch with me, Alejandra, as your teacher for the thirty days and thirty nights of

tradition, upon which time you will work toward your first accomplishment as a witch."

"*Na'am*," I answered, nodding my head for extra emphasis. I attempted to repeat the words as Alejandra had taught them to me, fumbling my way through the unfamiliar sounds of the language until I got to the end.

"*You will allow your companion, who has graciously led you to our world, to return to its home realm,*" she continued.

"*Na'am*," I said.

When I finished, Alejandra released my hands from hers to pick up the knife at her side. Even with my knowledge of what was to come, I still flinched when she sliced her wrist, smearing the blood into a little pool in the space between us. I held out one of my wrists for her to slit and gave my own blood sacrifice. I bit my lip, forcing myself to stare at the wound as the knife glided across my flesh. When she let go of my hand, I twisted my wrist around to let the blood drip onto the floor. Alejandra used the knife to swirl our blood together. When she lifted her knife, the glistening red pool soon moved on its own. The blood ran through the carved shapes on the floor, filling and illuminating the complex designs around us. When all shapes were full, the blood changed from red to gold, sparkling in the candlelight.

Alejandra grabbed my hands and recited more magical phrases. The candlelight dimmed as Alejandra's words summoned a new shadow into a circle behind her. When we ran through the ritual, she had told me that the shadow was another magical creature she would summon as part of my initiation. It was a friendly being, she said, like her version of a powerful companion that had been with her throughout her magical journey. The shadow whirled and twisted, never breaking out of the confines of the circle of summoning. It brought with it a strong gust of wind that blew out the candles and whipped past my ears, blowing my hair into the air.

Our only source of light was the lit designs, which somehow dimmed, leaving the room even darker than before. All I could do was stare into Alejandra's eyes while she continued to recite her phrases, even when I felt like wind was about to lift me out of my seat.

The shadow's movement and the wind slowed down. I only had a moment of silence before a new sound took its place. It sounded like a giant creature inhaling and exhaling deeply, each breath coinciding with a subsequent change in the shadow's shape. The more Alejandra spoke, rocking back and forth with concentration, her voice growing louder, the faster the creature breathed. I struggled to keep up with where we were in the ceremony. I lost track of what I was supposed to be doing and phrases I was supposed to say.

My brain tried to bait me with old feelings of regret for having left the safety of my home. I tried to fight against it. My heartbeat was no longer pounding with fear; it beat instead with the steady thrum of excitement and anticipation. This was the first step into my new life. And nothing and no one from my past could take that away from me no matter how much my mind wanted otherwise.

The creature inhaled. The pressure of the room changed, forcing all air out of my lungs. For a few excruciating seconds, my stomach and chest constricted painfully. I longed to take a breath, but I was unable to. My mind grew fuzzy and those few frozen seconds stretched out until it felt like this moment would never end.

Suddenly, the pressure changed in the opposite direction. A gust of wind flew back into the room from the sentient shadow. I tightened my grip on Alejandra to keep myself from getting knocked over. Relief filled me as I took in deep, hungry breaths, until I felt like I was going to start hyperventilating. Alejandra's focused eyes, the only constant through all this chaos, tethered me back to stability.

"*Khalas*," Alejandra said. "It is done."

The breathing ended and the shadow began to constrict. One by one, the snuffed candles flickered back to life. My companion hovered in midair. I could have sworn her eyeless stare was boring straight into my own eyes. She spread her tiny limbs into a star formation before disappearing slowly from my sight until she was nothing but a mirage that had only ever existed inside my mind. This part of the ritual, Alejandra had explained, was to set her free. Having fulfilled her purpose to bring me into this new world, she now returned to her original realm. I felt a pang of sorrow now that she was gone. *Goodbye.*

I remained where I was, heart racing. A new, unknown energy pulsed through my veins as I sat in silence, watching as the smile grew on Alejandra's face.

"Congratulations," she told me. "This moment marks the beginning of your journey toward becoming a witch."

We emerged from the basement. The energy within me grew stronger, working its way into every part of my being. It was like being filled. In that moment, I understood everything Alejandra told me. I felt a change coming over me, devouring what remained of my old self.

12

My life was forever changed. But this time, it wasn't because of something that had happened *to* me. It was my own decision; my own independence that led me to this stage. Nothing would ever be the same for me. This time, I held the power.

Shortly after the ritual, we ascended the stairs from the basement; the adrenaline drained from my veins. I felt as though every drop of energy was sucked out of my body. My legs were wobbly and my knees almost gave out. The only reason I didn't fall over was because Alejandra caught me.

"Ceremonies such as these can take a lot out of you," she said.

She walked me up to my bedroom before heading off in her own direction. I removed my robe and fell onto the bed. I imagined being back in the basement at the center of the ritual circle where Alejandra sat, my body filling with energy as I hovered above the ground and floated high enough to touch the ceiling. The ritual circle below me was lit with the fire of magic and I knew I could summon endless power if I wanted to. My initiation was only the beginning.

A wall of exhausted darkness took me into another round of dreamless sleep.

My mouth felt like cotton when I woke up the next day. I freshened up and slipped my robe back on before going downstairs to the dining room.

When I went down for breakfast, I found Alejandra already seated in her normal spot. This time, the delicacies I expected were replaced by fruit, plain rolls, and a pitcher of water. Alejandra sensed my surprise.

"The way to become a witch requires clarity of thought and purity of the body," she said. "Your diet for the remainder of your training will be very simple. The fewer distractions you have, especially anything physical, the better off your learning process will be."

I looked over the pitiful options set in front of me before I took a piece of fruit and a roll, washing it down with a glass of cool water, taking only a few minutes to finish my meager meal before beginning my true journey into magic.

ALEJANDRA and I sat in one of her rooms that seemed to exist to hold her book collection. The shelves were dotted with little trinkets that suggested journeys to faraway lands. We each sat on a cushion on the floor again and resumed our position from our ritual the previous night. I held up my arms with my palms facing outward, meeting Alejandra's hands. My eyes were shut but fluttered from the effort to concentrate. I took in deep, heavy breaths to match Alejandra's calm pace.

"Empty your mind," Alejandra told me right after instructing me to close my eyes.

"With each inhale, feel yourself taking in the energy from the world around you. Pull in the magic from my body into yours. Let the essence of your teacher strengthen you and guide you through your first day of study. With each exhale, imagine all discomfort, all doubt, all fear, flowing out of your palms and into me, where they will be neutralized. Let all memories of who you were before you decided to undertake this journey leave your mind. Let all weakness drain out of you, leaving behind only the best aspects of who you are as you build yourself into Dina the witch."

I struggled to follow along and do as she said. When I inhaled, my mind latched onto the incense, wondering about the scent, whether it was magical, what magic really was, which forms of magic Alejandra would teach me. By the time my lungs were full and I was ready to exhale, I couldn't get past the moments I wanted to forget. Those times when I had been frightened, fearful, helpless on the ground beneath Joe and Nameless, in my house when that creature tried to break through and even destroy my home. Those memories stuck to me, weighing me down like rocks in my pockets. I couldn't get into the flow Alejandra tried to create for me. I shook my head and opened my eyes, breaking the spell of the moment.

"I'm sorry, Alejandra, but I just can't do this right now."

I wanted to kick myself. I hadn't gotten to the interesting parts of having these new abilities and I was already messing up. If I couldn't master the simple stuff, how would I become the witch I yearned to shape myself into?

Alejandra could have cast me aside at that moment, ending my journey right there so she could pursue a more skilled candidate. Instead, she opened her eyes and tilted her head forward slightly, giving a small nod of understanding.

"It's alright, Dina. The aim of this exercise is to not only clear your mind in preparation for the magic that you'll soon practice, but to bring us together as teacher and pupil. It can be difficult when all of this is still so new to you. We'll practice this daily, and I can almost promise that it will become easier. And not only that, it may very well become the best part of your day." I couldn't see how sitting in silence and failing to meditate could ever rank as an activity that would get me excited to wake up in the morning.

"The journey of becoming a witch can sometimes be mundane, surprisingly," Alejandra continued. She stood up and walked toward the bookshelf, yanking a large tome from a tightly packed row of books before she returned to her seat. She cracked the book open, thumbed through to one of the pages in the middle, and began to read.

"A 'magic-free' society has never existed. Whether practiced in private or openly performed, magic has always existed in one form or another. Call us witches, warlocks, shamans, or sorcerers. Whatever you want to call us, there is no denying the place that we and our art have carved into every place throughout time.

The story of Siraj Ali and Zahrah, the founder of our kind, is present throughout the consciousness of our culture. The Adam and Eve of our magical folk transformed the desert around them into endless oases and created al-Alizab, a grand empire of magic, forging a center for all magical outcasts to flourish. The moment of their death marked the descent of their empire.

Most of their descendants had no vision for the empire. It was only in time that one of their successors, Tahani, was able to gather enough followers to form a new society of magic, 'al-Jafru'. She and her followers made repeated spiritual travels to bring magic to new heights.

Al-Jafru was not allowed to live in peace. Members of al-Alizab brutally attacked al-Jafru, igniting a conflict that would lead to the slaughter of too many of our kind. Following this bloodshed, our people scattered across the globe, immersing ourselves into whatever communities we could find. That is why witches and warlocks, in some form or another, can be found everywhere. Only the method of magic created by al-Alizab and al-Jafru is the purest form. All others are merely less powerful corruptions of this pure source..."

Images of dancing witches and warlocks clad in colorful

robes, holding hands and forming a circle, bounced across my eyelids. They were surrounded by endless dunes of golden sand. They began to chant words I couldn't make out. As they did, the sand within their circle blossomed into greenery. Leaves, flowers, and vines snaked up from the ground, weaving themselves into a structure that towered above them. I followed along as it twisted upward at an increasing pace. It was almost like it was trying to touch the sky...

Alejandra closed the book with a thud. My eyes popped open and I lifted my head from where it rested against the wall. I had been so soothed by Alejandra's narration that I had drifted away and let my imagination roam wild. I must have been exhausted if Alejandra's voice had been enough to make me doze off.

I made eye contact with Alejandra, expecting something like a reprimand for falling asleep. Instead, she remained silent, like she was waiting for me to say something.

What could I really say about the tome she read to me? I didn't understand half of the terms or the names, yet it had conjured such crisp images in my mind. Was it just my exhaustion, or was there something special about this story? Was I supposed to take this story as truth or was it one giant fairy tale?

"Where did that story come from?" I asked. "Is any of that true?"

One corner of her mouth formed a smile.

"Think of that story as an origin myth of our kind," she said. "Of witches. Though the truth may be shrouded in myth, there was likely a good pearl of reality that the story was based on. Regardless of its accuracy, I think you'll find great value in our mythology."

The cover of the book she was holding was maroon with shapes inlaid with shimmering gold. Most of the space on the front cover was taken up by a complex shape that reminded me of a miniature version of the circle we sat in the night before. Below that was the only letter on the cover I could make out; a giant "A." An *A* for Alejandra, perhaps?

Alejandra set the book back down on the bookcase and stood up. Her blue and purple robe and light hair spilled everywhere.

"Come," she said, holding her hand out to me. "Let's get started on the real part of your training." I took her hand and followed her through the hallway to my next lesson, wherever that might take me.

~

"SPELLS PROVIDE a way to channel the magic force running through our universe with your intent to create change in the world," Alejandra explained to me on my first day of practice. We were in another room in her house, this one was empty of everything besides another stick of incense burning in the corner. I was beginning to think I would never get that scent out of my nose.

We stood in the middle of the room with about a foot of space in between us.

"When casting a spell, you must also use your hand as a rod to guide this energy," she said. "Speak the spell's name clearly and correctly. What is the most important is the image in your mind of your intentions. A spell is only a word without your intent behind it."

She held her right hand out in front of her and raised it until it was leveled with her face.

"*Hariyak*," she said, moving her hand in a downward diagonal motion. She kept her hand suspended in midair, showing off her palm to me. My jaw dropped open as my eyes took in the flicker of flame roaring from her palm. She balled her hand into a fist. When she opened her hand again, the fire was gone, and her skin was the same brown it had been before, completely untouched by the fire she created.

"Why don't you try it?" she said. She snapped back into her position with her hand raised to her head. I mimicked her as closely as I could.

"Now remember, it's *hariyak. Har. Ee. Yak.*" She pulled her hand back down to repeat the motion a few times. I tried to copy her, mouthing the strange word to myself, trying to commit it to heart.

"Go ahead," she said. My lips trembled, some part of me still too afraid to speak that word even though I knew what it would do. What if I messed up, burned myself, or made Alejandra's house go up in flames? I mimed the motion one last time.

"Try it, Dina," she said. I raised my shaking hand into the air, swiping downward.

"*Har-Hariyak*," I said. I felt a jolt of heat in my hand but looked down to find nothing.

"Try it again," she said. I went back into position, moving my hand downward.

"*Hariyak*," I said, a little louder this time, moving my arm with increased speed. Still nothing. Not even a hint of warmth. What was I doing wrong? It looked so simple when Alejandra did it. What was I supposed to do to get this to work?

"One last time, Dina," she said. "Calm yourself first." My hand, now curled up into a fist, was shaking and my heart was pounding. I was almost certain if I looked in a mirror, I would see a sheen of sweat covering my face.

I closed my eyes, took in a deep breath of the incense-tinged air, and pictured a flickering flame in my mind, dancing in the darkness of my eyelids. I unclenched my fist and lifted my arm again, imagining the flame in my hand, pretending I could feel its warmth against my skin.

"*Hariyak*," I said, moving my hand back down again.

My mouth broke out into a smile. I opened my eyes and

looked down to find a tiny flare dancing around on my palm. Alejandra watched with pride. I couldn't believe I managed to do it on my first real attempt at magic. It all became so real to me in that moment; my future suddenly full of possibilities of what I could do and create if forming a little bit of fire in my hand was only the first step. I could only guess at what other wonders my lessons with Alejandra would hold.

13

———

Though my eyes were closed, I could see Alejandra's face as clearly as if I was staring right at her. Bright blue eyes and golden skin framed by waves of her blonde hair. She smiled and then opened her mouth to speak.

"Very good, Dina," she said. *"Your visualization is improving already."*

Her voice was somehow audible to me even though she wasn't physically speaking. We were meditating together again, just after our light morning meal. We sat cross-legged across from each other with our palms joined. Alejandra left out a plate for Lisa to join us during our meal, but she hadn't come down from her room all morning. Her constant absence weighed on me since breakfast, filling me with questions I wasn't sure I had the guts to ask.

"She can get like this sometimes. So fearful of the world outside. All she does is stay in her room, reading book after book. I keep telling her, if she wants to be a witch to the best of her abilities, she's got to go outside and practice. Even if it's just the backyard, or to one of our neighbors. They're trustworthy enough and I can still ensure her safety during times like these.

But as you could already tell, she was too nervous to even talk to you. I told her, she can't go through life being afraid all the time. But I can't control her every movement. I need to let her make her own decisions, even if they are to her detriment."

If that was true, if Lisa was truly afraid of going outside, too fearful to hold a conversation with an acquaintance of her mother's, I could understand where Lisa was coming from. Not too long ago that was the entirety of my existence. But wasn't Lisa a witch? She had the ability to change her reality. What could she be so afraid of that she would rather stay cooped up in her room than risk a conversation with a stranger, or venture outside? Had something happened to her that scared her into isolation?

When Alejandra left me alone for lessons, going into other parts of the house I had not yet explored, did she run up to her daughter to teach her magic lessons as well? Alejandra mentioned something about not wanting any harm to come to Lisa because some witch or warlock had a grudge against her. Is that what happened? Had someone with a fight to pick against Alejandra try to do something to Lisa? Or was Alejandra only afraid that this would happen because of her powerful position?

"You're worried," Alejandra said.

My mind had gone off the tracks yet again, destroying the vision Alejandra passed into my mind and replaced it with endless questions about things I didn't have the courage to ask her. It must've flown into her mind due to the connection between us. At the same time, I saw little point in trying to hide how I felt when Alejandra could clearly sense it. I kept my eyes closed while I continued speaking.

"It's just...Lisa," I said.

"Of course," Alejandra said. "Lisa is a seventeen-year-old, living in a world that most people couldn't imagine. Her father is long gone and has never been involved, so I've taken to raising her on my own. As a leader, you sometimes have to make decisions that not everyone agrees with. When I cast aside those two sadistic warlocks that would have killed you, it only put our entire community on edge. Lisa is undeserving of any of the punishments that they might prefer to inflict upon me by proxy. Some may even disagree with me on how I use my abilities, but I simply think that it is my gift to be utilized however I see fit. It's sad that I have to keep her so close but believe me when I say that my home is filled with enough wonders to keep her occupied for years to come."

Her bookshelves certainly contained enough. I wondered what she was referring to when she mentioned the other wonders in her home. What else did she have in this house that I hadn't seen?

~

ALEJANDRA'S daily lessons were a journey in unlocking newfound powers within myself, performing feats I never knew were possible for anyone, let alone myself, to carry out. In my previous life, as ordinary Dina Durst, my true abilities, my true purpose was completely locked away, and only something extreme could have broken the true witch within out of her shell.

After only five days of lessons, spending hours and hours in that same room, practicing the same gestures and syllables repeatedly until my mouth and arms were sore, Alejandra taught me how to summon all four elements.

Each day became a lesson in casting a new spell, learning them at a dazzling speed. First, we began with summoning small samples of each element.

Bahara for water.

Riyah for a burst of wind.

Sokrah for a mound of earth.

They each came with its own gestures to learn. For water, my fingers in both hands moved fluidly, for wind I rotated one of my arms at an exact angle, for earth I launched both of my fists toward the ground. At the end of each day, I stood amazed as I held a new element in the palm of my hand, the fruit of my hours of labored learning. They were never quite as large or as defined as the samples Alejandra created, but she always reminded me that was the result of years of practice. In time, I could learn how to perform magic stronger than hers. Though I doubted this would ever be the case, I was content for now to hold small samples of different elements in my hands. Though this might not seem like such a big deal to other witches and warlocks, I held these gems proudly as a concrete example of the power I was unlocking from within, the placeholder for grander accomplishments to come. I smiled to myself at the end of each practice as I remembered this was only the beginning.

THE DAY after we completed the basic elemental spells, Alejandra took me back to the same practice room and placed a smooth stone ball on the floor between us.

"It is quite easy to affect a small object with this kind of magic," Alejandra explained.

"Although more complicated than producing an element on its own, affecting other items takes the right amount of concentration on the item that you want to move and the spell that you must use to move it. Most mundane objects have nothing magical about them. No will to oppose your force. The situation gets a bit more complicated when you're dealing with charmed objects, even more so with people, but that's a lesson for a later date. For now, we're going to get started using this ball."

Alejandra looked down at the ball, curling one hand into a fist, while she lifted the other one above the fist, fingers spread wide.

"*Fawuk*," she said, raising her open hand into the air. As she did so, the ball lifted off the floor, floated in midair and climbed higher as Alejandra raised her hand. She held still when the ball was about level with her face.

"*Ila*," she said, lowering her free hand until the ball sat on the floor back in its original position. She pulled her free hand closer to her chest.

"*Nahu*," she said. The ball rolled toward her. She pushed her arm back out again.

"*Bayid*," she said. The ball rolled back, resting in its original place.

"You can try it now," Alejandra said. "Remember to focus on the object you want to move. Imagine it moving whichever way you desire. Concentrate the energy in your fist. Use your other hand to draw from that energy source and lift the ball into the air. Why don't you start by lifting the ball?"

I assumed the position as closely to Alejandra's as I could, squinting my eyes so that only the ball and the surrounding carpet were the only things in my field of vision. I mouthed the word silently to myself a few times before saying it aloud.

"*Fawuk*," I said.

The ball remained in its position. If I hadn't just started my lessons, I would have been discouraged enough to give up on the rest of the day. Then I remembered elemental spell casting had gone the same way at first. No matter how closely I tried to imitate Alejandra, or concentrate on the task at hand, it had taken me multiple tries before I was able to cast even the tiniest flame. What if the exact same thing happened in this instance? So, I took in a couple of deep breaths and tried again.

And again.

And again.

And again.

The ball stubbornly remained in the same position on the floor, almost taunting me for my inability to move it by will, even as I shouted the spell, and frustrated tears rolled down from my eyes. Why couldn't I get this damned thing to move? If I could create fire and water from thin air, why wasn't this spell a piece of cake?

Alejandra held her hand out, palm facing me, telling me to stop. She came toward me and placed both of her hands on my shoulders, looking me in the eye with her piercing blue eyes.

"Dina, you're trying too hard. Give yourself a break. Take a moment to remember why you're embarking on your journey. Focus on the bigger picture." I shut my eyes, letting the last of the warm tears flow down my face. I inhaled deeply enough to feel my chest and stomach expand.

Why was I here? I didn't come all this way to Alejandra's just to get frustrated by a lump of stone. I didn't survive my near-death experience, make it through an encounter with an otherworldly creature that crept out of my mirror, gone through the ritual with Alejandra, and sealing my fate as a witch in training just to end up crying.

In another timeline, I might still be lying in bed, fruitlessly trying to ignore my companion as she flitted around the room, too afraid to set foot into the real world ever again. But that Dina no longer existed to me.

Alejandra dropped her arms and resumed her position. I exhaled, opened my eyes again, and concentrated on the task at hand.

Even though magic was new to me, this didn't need to be an insurmountable obstacle. I had already taken part in a ritual and could create all four elements using only my abilities. I had a teacher with more power than I could imagine having. What was this spell but another small step, especially when compared to everything else I already endured becoming a witch worthy of being Alejandra's student?

So, I redid my pose and tried again.

And again.

And again.

Alejandra left the room to give me some time to focus on my own. I had no way of marking the passage of time and could only guess I practiced on my own for a couple of hours. My stomach grumbled. My head pounded for more nourishment. I made a deal with myself: no eating until I got this damn stone to move.

I took in another deep breath, feeling my tensed muscles unclench just the tiniest bit, and resumed the pose before trying again numerous times. Still no luck.

On the next try, the ball crept forward about an inch.

It was just an inch, such a small amount of space to move, but to me it meant everything. It meant my hours of work finally produced a worthy result. It meant I could get through this and all the unforeseen challenges this journey might throw at me. I could wield the kind of power I used to think was never possible for someone like me.

It all rested in my hands.

My bones ached, and for a fleeting moment, I found myself frozen. I was trapped in that field of grass, unable to do anything but watch the natural light around me change as I slipped in and out of consciousness. Something was touching my aching body. A do-gooder, trying to cover up my nudity with a jacket.

No, it was only a blanket. I pushed it aside and took a couple more breaths to calm myself. That night, that fear, those attackers, were all far away. I was in the best place I could be.

Slowly but surely, the rest of the room came into focus. I gently nudged my body forward, each muscle screaming in defiance with every movement. It felt like my muscles had been squeezed by something the night before, the aftereffects of an intense workout that never took place. Slipping on my clothes and brushing my teeth were a struggle. When I was clothed, I trudged down to the dining room, clutching my aching ribs.

"Did you sleep okay?" Alejandra asked me. I winced as I settled into my chair and my joints groaned from the effort. I did my best to nod. Though my stomach rumbled, I couldn't imagine the pain of moving my jaw to ingest anything.

"I feel like I got beat up," I said, regretting speaking from the pain it inflicted upon my face.

"These past few days have been a lot for you," she said. She stood up and lent me her hand. If I trusted her this far, I saw little reason to suspect anything right now.

She took me into another room with hardwood floors. She created and cast a simple circle made of chalk.

"Lie down in the middle," she said. I did as instructed, wincing again as I spread out my limbs so my hands and feet were just outside the circle. Alejandra grabbed something from a shelf and kneeled next to me, opening the container. She spread a thick blue paste over my arms, resulting in a tingling sensation and minty scent that soothed my pains.

"Using magic is like working a muscle," she explained, spreading the paste on my legs. "You can only practice so much before you wear yourself out, especially if you are in the beginning stages of learning. It's all normal. This will help you, at least temporarily, to avoid the *inhaka* that results from too much use. There's only so much that you can do to refill yourself, your energy, your *sahar* besides time and rest.

"You never seem to take a break," I said, closing my eyes and savoring the relief of whatever this magical mixture was. I could hear the smirk in her voice.

"I have been practicing magic for a long, long time, *habib*," she said, massaging my calves. "I have strained and regenerated myself more times than I can count." I imagined myself at that level of experience, able to go weeks of creating with magic without fatigue. One day, once my training was complete, I would get there. I just had to keep trying.

Alejandra granted me the day off and gave me a small vial of what looked like a liquid form of the blue paste to ingest throughout the day. By the next day, I felt new.

"A *shifaw*," Alejandra explained, holding a vial of the soothing liquid in the light for me to see how it swirled around the jar of its own accord. We were in a new room in her house. Her dedicated workshop; a room that was packed with musty, tattered volumes and cabinets full of mysterious ingredients stored in glass jars. Some of the items seemed to float or move slightly of their own accord.

"The traditional word for a healing potion," Alejandra explained. She set the jar back down amongst the ingredients laid out on her workbench. She pulled down a thin, tattered tome from the shelf above the bench and handed it to me.

"Many of the best potions are passed down in families. A colleague of mine gave me a copy of the recipe book that has been in his family for generations." Potion-making, as I learned, involved a lot more than gathering the right ingredients. Some of the components had to be raised, killed, or obtained during a certain point in the year or moon cycle.

"The quality of the ingredients they use, the caliber of your *nabat*, is crucial," Alejandra said.

"To become a skillful potion maker, you must memorize charts of nature and know the uses of hundreds, if not thousands, of ingredients, considering the proper incantations or rituals that must be performed to give the potions their effectiveness. It requires so much effort that certain members of our society specialize in creating the proper ingredients for the rest of us. But for right now, for you, there are only a handful that you need to know. Let's start with creating your first *shifaw*."

I flipped through the pages until I found the right recipe. Glancing from the page to the table, I compared each ingredient to its counterpart in the book. After measuring the correct portion of each ingredient, I ground the leaves as needed, and stirred the rest of the materials in a bowl. Finally, I finished by swirling some specially treated water into the mixture until its color resembled the hand-painted representation in the book.

I looked back up at Alejandra, searching her face for approval I was moving in the right direction. She smiled.

A thump coming through the wall right next to me and I jumped. But when I saw Alejandra had no such reaction, I figured I must've imagined it.

14

I saw myself from a third person's perspective, sitting cross-legged in the middle of a ritual circle. I could sense the presence of some other type of being nearby. A living shadow. As it crept toward me, it told me not to be afraid, it was only there to help me. And it whispered, somehow non-audibly, what its name was.

al-Nur.

"It means 'light' in the language of al-Alizab," Alejandra explained. Her words pulled me back into my physical presence, anchoring me to a solid reality.

"al-Nur is a being that has been with me for many years. Some witches may form bonds with beings from other realms of existence."

"Sort of like companions?" I asked.

"Yes, it's a similar idea to a companion. The difference is that these beings stick around for much longer than a companion does. The bond between such a being and a witch is much stronger. Think of it like the bond between a teacher and a student, such as you and me. I promise you lessons in power; you promise me devotion to the craft. As your instructor, the bond with al-Nur has been extended to you as well."

"But what exactly is al-Nur?" I asked. "Where did this being come from?"

"That is a more complicated question, but one that you will eventually come to understand. As you already know, there are other realms overlaid on our reality where other kinds of beings exist. *al-Nur* is one such being that has been around long enough to absorb plenty of magical knowledge and power. A being that isn't human but understands how matters work in our physical world, who wants to influence magic through the guidance of a witch."

I still wasn't sure I completely understood Alejandra's attempt to explain all of this to me, but I ingested the information regardless, holding onto the possibility this would all make sense to me by the end of my studies. If Alejandra summoned this being during my initiation, and she put her trust into it for such a long time, I figured I could live with the uncertainty for now and accept I would fully understand soon enough.

Alejandra continued the lesson later that day, when she brandished another large tome from a shelf of books and laid it in the space between where we sat on the floor. The spread she stopped at contained a series of plain circles with thick outlines on the left side, with more intricately drawn ones on the right side that was filled in with all kinds of designs. One of them reminded me of what the circle Alejandra and I sat in during my initial ceremony might have looked like.

"Rituals are the surest way to invoke powerful magic," Alejandra said. She flipped through some of the crisp, time-yellowed pages to show me additional variations on the circles from before, growing in complexity with each page.

"Many of them require great energy and concentration, complex incantations, and sometimes multiple people."

This form of magic should have been the most familiar to

me since I was introduced to it by Joe and Nameless the night of the attack. I wondered how long it would take for me to master this form of magic enough to use it for my own purposes. If they could do it with few preparations at hand, then maybe it was possible for me to do that as well.

"Even the most complicated of rituals begins with the simplest of steps: the casting of a proper circle to ground and organize your energy," she said.

She stood up and stepped away from the book, pulling a sheathed blade from one of the pockets in her robe. She pulled the blade from its covering and kneeled with her eyes closed. The blade was close to the floor and spun in a circle until she was back to where she started. I shuddered, remembering Joe did something like me, encircling me right before Nameless tried to destroy what remained of my physical body. That must have been what he was doing, preparing the circle for the ritual to come.

"Dina, are you alright?" she asked.

I shook my head, trying to shake off the remnants of the memory I wanted to forget, and moved my attention back to the book of ritual circles in front of me.

"Yes," I said. "I'm fine."

"The simplest rituals only require the minimum of creating an invisible circle around yourself," she continued. "For more complicated ones, you will need to actually draw a circle out or carve it into the space that you plan to use. You can then determine the specific purpose of the ritual by adapting the circle in various ways and drawing necessary symbols within the space."

"Just like in your basement," I said.

Alejandra nodded.

"Exactly," she said. "You can use just about any substance you have at hand, whether it be pebbles or sand or even ink, as long as your intention is there, and the shapes are properly made. The one that I just made is only temporary and won't last long, but you can feel it yourself if you move closer."

I took Alejandra up on her invitation and slowly reached one of my hands out toward her. When my fingertips were only inches away from touching her shoulder, I felt a warmth surrounding her, radiating up from where she had cast the circle on the floor. I could feel the warmth beginning to drain away, the temporary collection of magic dissipating back into the air. Alejandra smirked as I continued to wiggle my fingers around in the space.

Alejandra handed me the blade.

"Your turn," she said.

SOMETIMES YOU COULD INVOKE mystical beings when performing the proper rituals. This, as I learned, was exactly what Alejandra did during my initiation when she invited al-Nur, whatever that creature truly was, to partake in my initiation.

The lesson came after I followed Alejandra through a hallway. We passed by a couple of other rooms with locked doors. I thought I could hear distant muffles or someone shuffling around the house, noises that never became clearer no matter how long I tried to tune them into focus. Was it simply Lisa moving around the house? Surely the three of us must have been the only inhabitants in this place. Unless Alejandra kept other creatures here, the kind that she would teach me about later that day; her own personal menagerie. If that was the case, why couldn't she show them to me or at least explain the source of these sounds she surely knew I could hear? Maybe the noises weren't coming from anything living. With her experience with the craft, who knew what Alejandra was able to build.

The room had shelves on every wall, packed with books covered in a layer of dust. A small, empty table sat in the center of the room, surrounded by piles of trunks with locks. Alejandra knelt to one of the trunks and placed her finger on the metal clasp that had a small, raised spike in the middle. She barely flinched when it pierced her finger, leaving a small blob of blood behind when she removed her hand. A mechanism in the trunk steadily moved, like an unplugged machine coming back to life, then the top of it popped open.

"Our world is inhabited with creatures great and small, many unseen by the mundane eye, others created by our kind for particular purposes," she said as she dug around in the trunk, producing small bundles of rolled up papers she placed on the table. When she was done with the trunk, she stepped to the table to unroll some of them, revealing intricate drawings of beings that looked too fantastical to exist in the real world, creatures from old fairytales passed down from one generation to the next.

"Where did you find all of this?" I asked.

"I've spent a good deal of time in my life traveling from place to place," she said. "Exploring the origins of our kind. These materials were all scattered across the globe before I collected them. It's important for us to understand our roots, know the practices and beliefs of others of our kind. Traveling was its own teacher in a way. It shaped me into the witch that I am today. One day we can journey together, and you will create your own collection."

Finally finishing training, and joining Alejandra to sacred places, seemed like the kind of dream that excited me but would never come true. I pushed it aside and looked down at the scattering of drawings Alejandra placed on the table. Her hand swept from drawing to drawing, naming each of the creatures in turn.

Rafik: another name for our companions. Miniature beings

from an otherworldly place to assist new witches or warlocks. They resemble the fairies of ancient mythology. They had the same body plan; tiny bodies with wings attached and only a mouth for a face, but they came in a rainbow of colors.

I spotted one that reminded me of my own companion; a small blue creature with tiny wings and tiny claws, its mouth barely visible. A pang hit me in my chest from remembering my companion's appearance in my bedroom not too long ago, leading me to the path I needed to explore.

"And then of course there's *metluk*. But you're already far too familiar with that one. These beings of flame sometimes step into our world through the portals of mirrors or bodies of water. They feed off the energy that the soul of a witch or warlock can provide."

She pointed to a page that contained a series of drawings of flames emerging from different sources from a fountain or a mirror. Each drawing showed step by step how that lick of fire grew to form the shape of a humanoid being made only of fire. It brought me back to the night in my house when that thing came toward me, burning my carpet, and Kayla's denial.

"Not all creatures in our world are necessarily naturally occurring," she said, shuffling some of the drawings around in search of one in particular. She pulled out a multi-paneled page that contained drawings of what appeared to be small people trapped in jars, surrounded by scribbles that must have explained the magic mechanism behind them. I wondered how these miniature people related to what she just said.

"What do you mean? Like you can create life using magic?" I asked.

"Of sorts. To some degree, magic can be used to create creatures, beings without souls or intellect but who's function is based on pure instincts as decided by the witch or warlock that created it. Creatures like this. *Kadma*."

"What are they exactly?" I asked. "They just look like little people."

"Precisely. You have heard of voodoo dolls, correct?" I nodded. "This is a similar idea. Through a special process, you can create a miniature version of the subject for you to control. I'm not sure that I have seen anyone create one in a long while, though."

"Why not?" I asked. It sounded like an almost ideal way to control someone.

"The process is rare and difficult to carry out. Not all of our magical knowledge is stored in one place. Ever since we fled our homeland, our knowledge has become scattered. That is why I have made it one of my purposes to collect as much as I can and keep it all here. A treasury of our kind if you will. These here are different specimens of *kadma* that a warlock I once met had created over the years."

"What were they used for?" I asked.

"I'm not entirely certain. He kept that part to himself. But it probably wasn't for anything good."

I tried to imagine how it could be used, and all I could think of were bad things, keeping someone trapped against their will was worse than a slave. Alejandra gently pushed that image to the side and unrolled a long sheet of paper lying on the side of the table. Once unfurled, Alejandra kept one hand pressed against the top, the other hand pressed against the bottom, revealing the ghastliest creature I'd seen that day.

This creature was the color of the palest human I could imagine with long, sharp talons in place of fingers and toes. Its mottled wings were outspread, and it held its mouth wide open, revealing large, pointed teeth. It only had two slits for nostrils with big, black eyes above it.

"This is a drawing of a *saldan*. Back during the conflict between al-Alizab and al-Jafru, these were created by the latter to infiltrate the land of their enemies. They transformed some of their own kin into these creatures to fight the war for their freedom. Supposedly, they were powerful fighters in their original form, but they could also take the skin of other people, wearing the bodies of their enemies as a mask. As far as I know, no one has seen one of these since, so they are somewhat more mythological than the other beings that I have showed you today." She unrolled a couple sheets of paper that contained more interpretations of the same beast, none of which strayed too far from the first drawing.

"A witch created that?" I asked.

"Yes. Probably multiple witches and warlocks were willingly transformed into these beasts to give them fighting advantages. But the methods that they used have since been lost."

I imagined a witch like me voluntarily laying down in the middle of a ritual circle, surrounded by others in her coven. She felt each part of her body transforming as the magic ran through her. Her hands became claws and wings sprouted from her back. She emerged from the circle an evolved, powerful creature, strong enough to hide among and fight her enemy.

"Dina," Alejandra said, bringing me back to the present. "I must know, what do you think of all of this?"

"Of today's lessons?" I asked. She nodded. I looked up into her waiting face, blue eyes wide. I searched for the right words to explain how much my boundaries of what was possible had been expanded, brand new ideas for how magic could be used. There was more power in this world than I could ever have previously thought existed.

"I'm just...amazed," I said, failing to truly express the changes occurring deep within.

"I never knew that things like this could exist or ever be real. And the fact that someone of our kind could _create_ beings like this..." I shook my head.

"It's unbelievable in the best way. Inspiring almost. Like

now I have to re-imagine what 'impossible' really means. Or if 'impossible' even exists."

Alejandra's eyes filled with warmth, half of her mouth curling up into a smile.

"I want to show you something," she said. "Before, I wanted to wait until you were further into your training, but I now see that you are ready."

I helped her place the papers back into the trunk and followed her to another room in the house. She stopped at a room that had a symbol on the door, resembling a ritual circle. Alejandra placed her hand in the middle of it. I heard a click, and she pushed the door open.

The room we were in was almost dark. A sound like the silent static that comes from a television was coming from somewhere in the room, the same place that held the only source of light. A glass container, like a tank, filled with a transparent fluid surrounding something lying down. Another creature. Blue, human-like but with longer legs and arms with proportions that were all off. Its eyes, completely white, stared at the top of the tank. The creature was motionless, but I knew it must have been awake at least once.

"This is the thing that greeted me at the door," I said. I guessed it had called me down to breakfast the first night.

"Yes. This creature is my newest creation. My first successful foray into this world of creation." The thing in the tank still didn't move. I walked closer to the tank and placed my hands on the glass.

"You created this?" I asked. "But how?" How could she create something that walked and talked but wasn't human?

"I can explain to you in detail another time, after you have gained more understanding of how magic works, but the process was very complicated. I had to take parts from dead animals and create other parts using potions and spells. It doesn't have a brain, but I can get it to say and do basic things.

This creature is only alive and conscious in the same way that a jellyfish is. When I'm not using it, I store it right here in this potion mixture to keep it from decaying. Despite what others might say, I needed to journey in this direction. The magic world is getting too roiled up to be able to truly trust many of my kin anymore."

"What do you mean?" I asked, pulling my hands from the glass, and looking up at Alejandra.

"You must understand, Dina, the creation of many kinds of creatures, such as my experiment right here, are forbidden."

"Forbidden? Forbidden by who?"

"The magic world has always held its own rules for how our powers should be used," she said. "I would like to think that these taboos were originally created to prevent the conflicts that took place in the land of our origin from ever happening again. But, who's to say how you can and cannot use the abilities that were naturally given to you? I see them only as unnecessary restrictions, though I am certainly in the minority with that belief. That is why I must keep some aspects of my work to myself."

Everything was falling into place of why Alejandra was so secretive of her work, why she always kept me and her daughter inside. She had the creativity and courage to create what others could not, and some of the community would have hated her, or were even envious of her to the point of violence for the lengths she was willing to go to. I felt as though she had given me a treasure.

"You must see it the way that I do," she said. "This is just another way for us to wield our power. I don't believe that anyone or anything should be able to hold us back."

I stared back at the blue creature in wonder and amazement before we left the room. As I walked back up to my bedroom, and parted ways with Alejandra, I wondered what other spectacles she held in other rooms. Could other creatures, creations of Alejandra's, be responsible for the noises I sometimes pretended not to hear?

As I fell asleep that night, I imagined myself drinking a potion and emerging as something more powerful. A chimera of the creatures Alejandra taught me about that day. Clawed hands, wings at my back, pale skin, spreading jets of fire from my body, towering over everyone else. No one could stand in my way. Not the witches or warlocks at the carnival who had demanded my sacrifice until Alejandra arrived. Not Joe. And certainly not Nameless, for whom I saved a special treatment for, clawing and destroying them until they were nothing more than a bloody pulp, a fate more gracious than what they deserved.

15

W*hy me?* I wondered during one of our meditation sessions. She had a coven full of witches and warlocks, people who had been raised from birth to utilize their magic force. Yet, I was her only student. After my head flooded with images that were not my own, I realized I must have wondered too loudly. Alejandra heard me, and this was her response.

I was sitting at a dining table sitting across from two people I didn't recognize. One was a middle-aged man with dark brown skin, who sat there shaking his head at something unknown. The other one looked amazingly like Alejandra, if only a shade or two darker. The air was heavy with tension; so much so, I barely touched the plate of food in front of me. The woman was staring at me, breathing heavily. I felt like I was placed in the middle of an argument.

"*La hija del diablo!*" she shouted, grabbing the cross that hung around her neck. "You fill me with disgust. Get out of my sight!"

"Maria!" the man said, finally participating in the scene. "Please, calm down!"

"No. No daughter of mine will turn her back on the Lord and fill herself with darkness."

She pushed up from the table and headed toward me. I jumped up and left, sprinting up the staircase into my room. Even with the door shut, I could still hear the woman shouting in a mixture of Spanish and English. I fell onto my bed, sinking my face in a pillow and covering my ears to block out the rest of the world. It wasn't long before I pulled my face out of the pillow to find I had left a moist outline in the shape of my face on it. Tears. I opened my mouth and let out a scream so loud and strong, it scratched my throat.

Darkness.

I came back into my true present, my heart heavy from the scene I witnessed. I was hesitant to open my eyes out of fear the tears would come pouring down if I did. My palms remained against Alejandra, though she had already ended the scene she wanted to share with me. The memory was so personal that I almost couldn't believe she had shared it with me. For the first time, I had a glimpse of the world through Alejandra's eyes, and I didn't find what I expected.

"Dina, you are the first student that I have taken in," she said. "When you visited the magical gathering with your companion right beside you, lost and fearful, I knew that I had to help you out of your predicament. We are linked through our shared pain. No one in your life believing what you're going through or thinking that it is evil. Outcast from the community that is supposed to be your home. Stumbling into a journey that you had never asked for with little initial guidance. I have felt similar pain before I shaped myself into who I am today. I did not want to only tell you this. I wanted you to feel my *why* for becoming your teacher."

I opened my eyes, finding them misty.

"The devil's daughter," I whispered, gazing at the floor. "I can't believe it. How old were you?"

"I was a teenager," she said. I looked back up at her face. "Not much older than Lisa, in fact. It was al-Nur, the being that was present at your initiation, that led me to the path that I now walk today, made me understand that though I might have been an outcast among most people, I was a member of a special community that would greatly appreciate all that I had to offer. No one believed me, and when they did believe me, they treated me as if I were tainted. These memories of pain may hold us down, like stones in water. But we, Dina, have the ability to transform that pain into power. Never forget to channel your tragedies into potential as much as you can. Make use of the injustice that has befallen you. When life gets difficult, it may be the only way to empower yourself to make it through. The guidance of al-Nur is what has allowed me to endure the trials and tribulations that stood in the way of all that I've ever wanted to do to where I am now and to the throne of where we will sit in the future. Trust me as I trusted al-Nur and together we will march toward the venerated destination where we belong."

THE REVELATION CAME to me toward the end of my training, found in the same book that Alejandra gave me with our creation myth:

The secret that al-Jafru discovered formed the basis of the most powerful kinds of magic in existence:

Blood.

What could be more symbolic of humanity's unique energy than the blood that courses through our veins and gives our bodies sustenance? Giving blood creates an unbreakable bond, powers your magic in a way that nothing else can. Just as blood magic can have more potent effects than anything else, one must remember that its consequences can also be far more dire...

All this time, I tried to think of what I wanted to do with Joe and Nameless once I finally got ahold of them. I suddenly realized I had no reason to waste my precious revenge solely on leaving them for dead. I could take their lives, not only for vengeance, but a greater purpose. If it was true there were no ingredients more powerful than the blood and the soul, it only made sense to make some use of theirs.

I revealed my intentions to Alejandra via meditation.

"Turning your revenge into a blood magic ritual to help you advance?" Alejandra said, after I showed her my intentions through meditation. "Superb. I'm sure you must be beating your mind trying to figure out a way to properly perform this ritual."

I nodded my head.

"Excellent. We have much to discuss. I've got to get you prepared if you want to do this ritual correctly."

MY NIGHTLY MEAL would often consist of a slightly more filling spread of breads and an assortment of jams while Alejandra quizzed me on whatever topic my lesson was that day. Tonight's review was interrupted by something banging on the front door. The blue creature came back into the room, thudding with every step, saying something that was too indistinct to understand into Alejandra's ear.

"At this hour?" Alejandra asked. She got up and walked to the door, the blue creature trailing behind her. I could hear muffled shouting from the other side.

"I'm no longer allowing visitors," Alejandra said. "You should know that."

"Gideon sent me!" a voice on the other side said, followed by more indistinct yelling.

"Very well. But if you would please calm yourself first." The noise quieted down.

"Let him in," she said, presumably to the creature. She came back to the entrance of the dining room.

"I'm so sorry, Dina, but I must handle this in private," she said, before closing the dining room door and departing back down the hallway. She didn't have to spell out for me what she meant. I stacked my utensils on top of my plate and watched as it sank into the table and disappeared within seconds before getting up and heading toward my bedroom.

On my way back to my room, I heard voices, which grew in volume until I came across a door that had been left slightly ajar. This must be where Alejandra and her guest were conversing. I knew I should have kept walking to my room and ignore the temptation of wanting to listen in. Who knew what they were talking about? What if I heard something I wasn't supposed to know? I still had so much to learn about how this world worked. Despite the potential dangers, I was too drawn to the conversation going on inside to follow what my common sense told me.

"We're in too deep now," the visitor said. A deep male voice, the gruffness of someone middle-aged. I peeked my head into the smallest crack in the doorway just enough for me to get a glimpse of what was happening without revealing my presence.

"Why did Gideon send you?" Alejandra asked. The man, dark skinned and stocky, blabbered an incomprehensible mess. His leg bounced up and down, tapping against the floor.

"Take a deep breath. Tell me what happened," she said.

"You know I don't mean no harm, right? I'm just passing through with the rest of my coven. Gideon told me to go with Rahim this time. Ya gotta go where the markets are. We make some of the finest *nabat* anyone in this area has ever seen. And now _he_ wants in on it. We used to trade before with some of his folks, way back in the day. But then they just fell off the map. I don't know how he found me, *malika*. I thought we did a good enough job covering our tracks. I never meant nobody no harm. But he found me and"

"Slow down, Bodhi. Tell me from the beginning."

"We just rolled into town to sell our shit at some of these markets, right? Connect with a few of the smaller covens. Maybe make some new contacts. We heard the rumors about the two warlocks who almost screwed up everything for us, but that was all over, right? I should've known something was wrong when that *ayidi* crashed into that gathering here. Shit's turning all upside down. I ran into him one time before at a different market. He was just a little thug trying to hustle, nothing to be worried about. I don't know what happened, Alejandra. He's got people following him now, doing whatever he says. They found Sahir a couple days ago, carved him up and sent him back to Gideon with a message. He's gonna figure out where our farm is where we make all of this. He...he said that he's only gonna give us one chance to take his offer where he'll still give us a cut. But just a sliver! After all that we've gone through to get the business to where it is, busting our asses, not sleeping, traveling across the country...he's just gonna take it from us, just like that. It's like everyone's so desperate these days. I've seen some shit, but I've never seen it this bad. You can't trust nobody!"

I couldn't believe it; a man of his age, and apparent stature, began to cry. He shoved his face into his hands, shaking his head back and forth like he was trying to will away the story he was telling out of existence. Alejandra leaned forward and placed a hand on his shoulder while he heaved with tears.

"...Abeer," Alejandra said, shaking her head.

"You know this asshole?" Bodhi asked, lifting his face from his hands.

"I've heard the stories. This wannabe coven leader needs to learn his place," Alejandra said, shaking her head again. "Too many of these idiots getting a glimpse of what our trials have produced, and they think that they deserve it all to themselves."

"Sahir said that they put something on him," he continued. "Some kinda cream or some shit when they were done cutting him up. He said it was the worst pain that he'd ever had, and you _know_ what kinda shit that bastard's been through. Said it felt like he was in it for an eternity. Even when he was talking about it, he was shaking. And he was crying. Sahir, _crying_. He doesn't even want us to try to put up a fight. He wants us to just bend over and take it, just like that."

"It's like he came out of nowhere. I'd heard some rumors about him back when I was in Greenfield, you know? But people said that he was just a street thug peddling low quality shit. The next thing I know, he's coming after Sahir and the rest of us _our_ witches and warlocks, _our_ people, _our_ product. Rahim said we can't just go home now. We gotta figure this shit out first, or else he'll just keep coming after us. My coven wasn't even large to begin with. You know why I got into all of this. I just wanted to provide for my family, Alejandra, and now he's coming after me. I can't- I can't do this, Alejandra. What if he finds my family? Where am I supposed to go? What am I supposed to do? Gideon sent another one of us to Saida up in Riverside; her coven has helped us out before. But this time, they won't even bother. She said that they have enough infighting of their own to deal with. It seems like everybody's beefin' these days." He put a hand on his forehead and slid it down his face.

"But that's not the only reason why Gideon sent me here. We...he and Rahim think they've found the Source." I don't think I've seen Alejandra look as taken aback as she was just then. She leaned in closer to Bodhi.

"The situation in Fairview, especially downtown, it's getting worse. You see people injecting _saharil_ left and right. Stealing. Pulling tricks. Working with some of the worst enchanters imaginable. He thinks...he thinks that's how Abeer got to where he is. He's been peddlin' this shit from the start. All of his followers, they're too terrified to have their supply cut off, so they'll do anything he says. People I've known forever, they're like zombies now. It's worse than any *ayidi* drug that I've ever seen. Gideon says that you were right to ban it when it first started coming in."

"It still trickles in from time to time," Alejandra said. "Some of us can't resist. But Rahim, what makes him think that he's found it? From what I've heard, many others have tried, and they've either failed or stumbled into something that got them killed."

"One of Abeer's acolytes. Rahim got a hold of him, helped him get clean. He started spilling the secrets. Rahim had some of us follow the trail to see where it led. It's gotta be somewhere in Greenville he thinks."

Alejandra gave a loud sigh and shook her head.

"If it's in Greenville, then I wouldn't get my hopes up. We all know the wretched hive that has sunk its claws into that city."

"That's why Gideon wants to work with you," Bodhi continued. "We can't do this alone, especially not with Abeer on our asses. We need your coven and your knowledge. Gideon wants to share the spoils."

"I won't believe it until I hear it straight from his mouth. Why would he send a goon to give me such an important message?"

"Because if I die, it won't make much of a difference," Bodhi said. "But if some bastard witch or warlock got their hands on Gideon...the coven needs him. Our community needs him. Just like the community here needs you. He's holed up too, nice and safe he says, but he won't tell me where. He can't afford to leave."

"Bodhi," Alejandra said, putting her other hand on his left shoulder, "You've come to the right place. I can help you. And I can assure you that this hoodlum won't be a problem for you much longer."

"Your coven can help? You would do that for us?"

"Bodhi, you and your circle have been one of the best providers of *nabat* that I've ever come across. My elixirs would not be nearly as powerful without your endless work. Abeer is just a boy who wishes that he had the power of a real leader, and he'll intimidate and threaten until he gets what he wants until someone stops him. I'll have him taken care of. As long as you comply with the terms of our deal."

"Yes, of course. I would never think to break our terms. You're the only resource I have left. You'll have my services, our services, whenever you need. When we're safe again. When I know that I can walk outside without him coming after us."

"Very well," she said. She stood up and opened one of the cabinets in the room. Her hands emerged with a glass jar full of a boiling, pinkish liquid. She transferred the jar to Bodhi's shaking hands before clasping both of her hands around his. His shaking seemed to minimize just the tiniest bit.

"Take this with you," she said. "It will be good for Sahir's recovery for when you return to your coven." Bodhi looked down at the jar with wide, amazed eyes.

"I- I really can't thank you enough. You've looked after us when no one else would. You've kept our operations going."

"It is my pleasure," she said. "We shall see to this soon."

Bodhi got up from his chair and they walked toward the door. For a split second, I could have sworn Alejandra's blue eyes connected with my own. I sprinted toward the staircase before Alejandra noticed me, or more importantly, my eavesdropping. When I was almost at my destination, I bumped into Lisa in the hallway.

I was too startled to say anything. For one long, frozen moment, we stood motionless before each other. She cast her eyes down and, without a word, shoved past me, heading in the direction I just came from. I practically sprinted the rest of the distance to my room.

In my solitary silence, I allowed myself to doubt Alejandra for the first time. Yes, she saved me and taught me a new and improved way to live, but did I really know who this woman was? The strange ambient sounds that came and went and the conversation I just overheard made me think otherwise. I could just leave, couldn't I? Why did she want me hidden from her visitor? I considered leaving altogether, running through multiple possibilities of my next course of action.

I COULD HARDLY CONCENTRATE during my lesson the next day. My stomach churned too much for me to even try to keep anything down when I tried to eat breakfast. When Alejandra spoke, I felt like I was interpreting her words through a thick fog that coated my mind. I couldn't stop shaking my leg even when I was supposed to be silently reading.

She knew, didn't she? She knew I listened to her conversation. She was just waiting for me to admit it. She was going to let me suffer with my own guilt until I finally came clean.

My hands were shaky against hers when we returned to our daily meditation. I felt my mind slip in and out of focus. Flashes of a woman veiled, walking across the scorching sands of a faraway desert, trailed by a couple of others pulling what appeared to be a wheelbarrow full of something I couldn't make out. Another flash of her blowing the dust off the cover of a thick tome, the weight of the leather and paper heavy in her hands. Now she was slipping into a maze-like tunnel beneath the Earth, crawling through to discover a hidden space filled with coffins. The space was not tall enough to stand up in. The woman knelt and crept toward the furthest coffin, shoving the cover aside with her palms to reveal...

I shook my head and the vision disappeared, pulling my trembling hands back into my lap.

"Dina, what's wrong?" Alejandra asked, furrowing her brow. "These are very special moments to me that I haven't been able to share with anyone else. Not even with Lisa quite yet." I felt too dishonest to look her in the eye, so I stared at the space beside her head.

"Clearly, you're struggling with something," Alejandra said, leaving a silence for me to respond. I didn't say anything.

"I know you heard my conversation."

I waited, with my heart racing, for her to say something else. To finally punish me for overstepping my boundaries. I prepared myself for the worst. Maybe she would throw me out for good, and I'd have to stumble back to my crumbling old life all because I made a stupid decision.

"And I know that you must be curious," she continued. She placed both hands on my shoulders and looked me squarely in the eyes. I saw no anger. Only genuine concern. I felt like I was finally able to breathe again.

"The magic world here...it's getting worse. There wasn't ever a time when we could co-exist peacefully, but these days it's like an all-out war in some places. This coven wants that coven's spells, or that coven's secret ingredients, or some scrap of supposedly sacred magic that could finally bring them abundance. It's a battlefield out there sometimes."

I thought back to the recent crime wave I heard about on the news, warnings to young women on their own to start carrying pepper spray in their purses and to never walk at night alone. Classic advice that was hammered into our heads even more recently, but I now understood why. This wasn't gang warfare or some false flag conspiracy. There had been a whole society, an entire world, going on around me. It was all invisible to me until now.

"There was a time when it looked like it was starting to get better, as if we could share instead of fighting. I was a part of that. I have helped a lot of people here. Just like how I want to help you." I had no proof she was lying, and I felt too guilty to continue doubting her after everything she did for me.

"I'm not the only leader in this world," Alejandra said. "Some of them call me *malika*. Queen. Captain. I keep the coven here bound together for the greater good. That is my job. But it's never been secure and never will be. I can only imagine that the next time an 'Abeer' comes around, his next target might be me. It could be happening already, especially with all that I'm trying to accomplish here. Now, I trust Bodhi. And for that matter, I trust Rahim and their *malik,* Gideon. But loyalty... it can be bought or sold for the right spell or charm in this world. Besides, some others might disagree on what we call progress. That's why I've had to turn inwardly, you see. I can't put Lisa at risk and I have to be so much more careful with the witches and warlocks I associate with. I can't let any harm come to my student. But everything here in this house..." she gestured toward the ceiling, moving her index finger in a circle.

"I've put my very blood into keeping it safe. And though there's many whose loyalty I can't ever be certain about, there are a few who have proven their trustworthiness."

"A coven is supposed to be a family. Someday I would like for all of us to return to that. Starting with you. My purpose here is to build a community as strong as the full extent of our abilities, even if it seems like it's all falling apart out there. You too should have a purpose in your studies to guide you. I encourage you to think of one, but you should let the purpose come to you."

~

My purpose occupied my mind for days afterward, crowding out the numbing thoughts that permanently latched themselves onto my brain. I meditated on it whenever I got the chance. An answer finally arrived midway through training in a spell casting, which left me feeling increasingly exhausted at the end of each day. After a time, the fatigue, the studying, and the meditation swirled together to provide me with a new state of mind. I experienced a clarity that helped me weed out my destructive thought patterns.

On the edge of sleep, I saw myself being beaten and violated all over again. And then, I saw myself taking a backseat to everything else in my life, giving up on what few goals I used to have. All I wanted to do was lie in bed and retreat to a world where my daily pain did not exist. But why? Why had I become a bystander in my own life?

I could place the blame on those two men: Joe and Nameless. The damage they did to me was irreparable. Almost everything I did since was in response to the fear they forced into me. But why should I let them have the final say in what I did with my life? Shouldn't they be the ones suffering for that night? I would no longer be the helpless one. They would cower in fear first. I knew I found my purpose. My eyes opened from pre-sleep.

The goal of my magic study was to become less helpless. The first step was carrying out my own justice to those two men.

PUTTING my purpose into a concrete statement made it possible for me to go through my training with a new sense of comfort. I had a specific goal I wanted to work toward. Every action I performed and piece of knowledge I gained were stepping-stones to help me get there. The food felt less lacking, the meditation easier, and the studying more efficient when I put everything into this perspective. I was not only growing into a witch, I was becoming a stronger person.

I did not have to tell Alejandra my purpose. During one of our daily meditations, my purpose flowed effortlessly from my mind into hers. I suddenly saw myself roaming through the world, casting whatever spell I pleased, fully powerful. I had become a weapon of magic. A *saldan*, as they were described, creatures with mottled yellow skin, long claws on every digit, wings to carry them from one destination to the next, and the darkest eyes that would strike fear into anyone they encountered. A *saldan* could take on the skin of other humans and use them as a disguise against their hideous exterior. As one of these creatures, nothing and no one could hold me back as I sought my violent revenge.

My vision concluded with finally finding Joe and Nameless, twisting their existence into worlds of pain. Alejandra suddenly breathed in sharply, destroying the calm we created together and sent my vision floating into the ether.

"Dina," she said, after looking into my eyes for an extended moment. "You are even more determined than I thought."

From then on, my training from Alejandra became more defensive than instructive.

Sarifa to deflect a spell. It doesn't always work on every spell, Alejandra said, but it was usually worth a try.

Kafada to slice into flesh.

Alama to cause a brief burst of pain.

If I was too drained to continue that day, Alejandra reminded me to think of my vision. It always gave me enough energy to continue with full force. We continued meditating together for longer periods of time. The more we meditated, the closer the messages between us grew, until the images she passed into me became as clear as a movie.

During one of my final days of training, Alejandra began our meditation with a disclaimer.

"Dina, I've decided that I want to show you something special today," she said.

"Something that I have not shown to anyone else. I want to show you because I want you to be a part of this. You have more raw power than any witch in training that I have met. I want you to think of this as the introduction for what is to come."

I closed my eyes and concentrated on my breathing until it matched the pace of Alejandra's. Her vision became my own, although I could still feel the vision's foreign quality at the edges of mind.

Alejandra and I stood together, wearing magnificent, billowing robes. Warmth and pride radiated from my body. We walked from one city to the next with impossible speed. No matter where we went, I was overwhelmed with an intense peace and calm as all my previous fears melted away into insignificance. In each city, we were surrounded by our own kind. As we walked through the streets, other magical folk joined us, becoming our followers. I felt blissful. Tranquil. At home. I finally found my place. The vision became a dream from which I never wanted to wake.

"We didn't have to hide ourselves," I said after the vision ended. I looked into Alejandra's comforting eyes. "We could do, and be, and make...whatever we wanted."

"Precisely. Our kind has existed in a stalemate with the ordinary world for too long. We have this tradition of keeping ourselves hidden, but why should our kind shrink away from this ordinary, inferior world? I have found a way to raise our kind to a new level of existence. With this new freedom, we shall shape the world as we see fit. We will have the power at last. With your strength and the support of my network within this community, I know that we'll be able to make this vision into reality. I know that you have your own reasons for undergoing your training to become a witch, and I fully support you in fulfilling your purpose. I only ask that after you're finished training, and after you've sought your well-deserved revenge, that you never forget the greater goal that I have created for us. As soon as you return, we will be able to begin."

I couldn't say no to her even if I wanted to. All I could do was nod and try to fight back the inexplicable tears the vision created. I never saw my life as part of anything grander than the ordinary.

"This is amazing," I said to Alejandra, an understatement of my true emotion. But that felt like a barely adequate response, so I followed up with something more.

"I promise," I told her. "To never lose sight of the greater goal."

16

On the morning of my final ritual, I allowed my thoughts to swirl around me while soaking in a tub of warm water, surrounded by incense and steam. Small red rivulets spiraled out from my torso into the surrounding bath water from the incisions on my body, drawing a new design for my own purpose. I grimaced at first from the pain as Alejandra helped me carve into my own flesh. Even sitting in water made it throb. Now I relished the feeling. Old scar tissue was reinvigorated and made anew, part of my plan to create a more powerful version of myself. I ran my plan through my mind, eagerly awaiting the moment I was able to launch into action.

The sacred basement was much the same as it had been the first time I experienced its brilliance. Alejandra and I took our places in the same individual circles as before. She clasped her hands around mine as we had done so many days in meditation.

"You will be granted the power to fulfill your intentions and beyond," Alejandra said, speaking the sacred language of magic. *"But you must remember the sacred bond between teacher and student, indebted to one another for life."*

"*You must show us your intentions for undertaking this journey,*" Alejandra said. I painted a clear picture of my revenge in my mind until it filled every fiber of my being, reaffirming my confidence in what was to come.

"*State them aloud for the universe to hear,*" she said.

I transformed my thoughts into words. As I completed my statement, Alejandra grabbed the knife beside her and cut into her arm, spilling her blood into the circle. I then embraced the weapon and accepted the infliction of pain upon myself, seeing it as a small price to pay for my grander plan.

Our voices speaking as one, Alejandra and I chanted the incantation that would bring the powerful entity back into our world. My excitement, but not my fear, grew as the wind picked up and charged around me in every direction.

Just past Alejandra's head, an entity took on an earthly form in its place in the circle. The only thing visible was a dark cloud expanding that seemed to have generated from nothing at all. It remained a fuzzy mass that struggled to exist, never taking on a true shape even after it had stopped expanding. Yet, it exuded an intense power from its mass. I focused back on Alejandra's face as it began to "breathe". Together, we chanted another set of ancient words. With every inhalation, I could feel more power rushing from the entity and into me. I felt so much power, I was ready to scream.

I watched, horrified yet excited, as a portion of the dark entity stretched out from its place in the corner and slithered toward my body, coating every inch of my body in its mysterious black mist. Alejandra's eyes were my only support before the darkness covered everything. My head pounded with strange, foreign thoughts. I listened to them as the dark coating shrunk closer to my skin.

The thoughts did not come in words but images. The entity, whatever it was, was trying to show me its next move, foreshadowing the pain I would soon experience. Before the pain began, it allowed me to see an image of the end result, granting me the strength to endure the next step.

The mist solidified and constricted me until I could barely breathe. It forced my mouth open and flowed into me. No amount of anticipation could prepare me for the excruciating sensations of the process. My skin felt like it was being torn from my body, cell by cell. I wanted to scream in anguish louder than I ever had before. My body jolted with bolts of electricity; my skin felt like it was on fire until I emerged from my old skin. I was vulnerable, yet free.

For just a moment, I felt a bit of pain now that my body was exposed to the empty air around me. My body shifted and changed in reaction to its new exposure. My limbs grew or shrunk to new and unnatural proportions while I thrashed around on the floor, helpless against the transformations being performed on my body until the pain ended.

I looked at my old body from my new perspective. The old Dina was sprawled out on the floor, while I had become this strange, new creature. My new form was yellow and mottled, my fingers replaced with long claws and wings sprouting from my back. I could only imagine that my eyes were as dark as the creature we summoned.

A *saldan*.

"Revenge," the entity told me, suddenly shifting its form of communication from images to broken sentences. "Any...form. Free...no shell." The sound of breathing slowly began to leave the room, and with it, the presence of the entity.

"*Khalas*," Alejandra said, signaling the end of my official initiation into magic.

I was granted a new and unexpected freedom. Free to be whatever I wanted. Do whatever I wanted.

Despite all the power I was given, I wanted to be surrounded by the comfort of being back in my own skin again. I scampered back over to my body, taking a good look at my old, hideous self, lifeless beneath me, bloody wounds just beginning to congeal. In that moment, it became everything about me I wanted to leave behind. It no longer defined who I was. I could enter or leave it as I pleased.

I stood over my old shell and imagined myself taking on its exterior as my own, only a temporary vehicle for arriving at my final destination. Within moments, after only blinking, I was back within my old body. I pushed myself up, nearly hyperventilating from the experience, wiping some of the sweat off my brow and shaking from the aftershocks of agony. Alejandra was beaming with pride.

"Congratulations, Dina," Alejandra said. "You are now a witch." She handed me the ceremonial knife we used in the ritual.

"Now you shall fulfill your purpose."

17

Scrying didn't always work. It was a method of supernatural sight, usually achieved by concentrating over a specially treated mirror or pool of water. It was usually only possible to locate a person's general vicinity if the scryer had a strong emotional connection to them. Even with that criterion, it didn't always work. I was determined to try anyway.

Alejandra prepared the bowl of water for me and then left me. I had since changed into the silk robe she gifted me; a sibling of her own robe swirled with purple and blue that instead combined hints of red and yellow, like a flame growing across the fabric. A new power forming. A new life began. The official garb of a new witch.

By now, I learned how to make the anger and anguish serve me instead of lashing me around at its whim. Remembering my broken body and my broken spirit, the destroyed soul I was only months prior. The physical pain I had to endure day after day. The disbelief of my own family when I had tried to tell them the truth. The faces of those two damned men. Sure, they were branded and banished. But that was not enough punishment for what they did to me.

I hunched over the bowl of water until my vision went blurry, filling myself with the red-hot anger evoked by memories of that night. I stared until I thought I saw images and shapes form, but that turned out to be merely tricks of the light and my exhausted eyes.

Whether from memory, magic, or simply strained eyes, I saw myself reversed into a younger woman. My parents calling me the worst words possible, filling me with shame. Next, I was trudging across an empty desert, body aching and mouth dry, but with a determination that nothing could vanquish. The insides of beautiful, palatial-like structures that held the contents of an entire imagination.

But these were not my memories. These were the visions Alejandra shared with me, the beginning of her great story. After stretching my limbs, I settled back into position. Something told me I had a little further to go. I needed to push myself a little more, ignoring my aching body and the doubting thoughts trying to cloud away everything else. That kind of thinking was part of my old life. That was the part of me I wanted to leave behind when I embraced what I was truly becoming, what I was meant to be.

Hours later, something came into focus. I saw a vague, stick figure-like shape. The more I focused on it, the sharper the image became. A person. A man. As the details filled in, the familiarity of the figure grew until the resemblance of the face was unmistakable. Walking from one indistinguishable place to another, until the details around him settled into a concrete pattern. Though not exact, this was enough to point me in the direction of where I needed to go next.

An unknown melody came to me and escaped my lips as the image became as crisp as a photograph. I jumped up from the bowl of water, running through the hallway until I heard Alejandra's voice. When I cracked open the door, I found her standing before a mirror. But what was reflected in the mirror was not herself. Instead, an older man responded to an unheard question Alejandra must have asked him.

"Thank you for taking Bodhi into your care," he said. "I am sure that the elixir you shared will do quite well for Sahir's injuries when Bodhi is able to return. I'm looking forward to seeing what you can create once we get a hold of some *saharil*."

"Gideon, you know that it won't be as simple as just setting foot into Greenville," Alejandra said. "Even with the best of both of our forces. Gathering whoever we can trust these days. We would have to keep it a simple operation."

"Trust me, my witches and warlocks are loyal," he said. "If they wanted to run off and chase a dragon, they would've done that already. I think we're already past that point."

"While I'm relieved to hear that you can say that so confidently, I've learned that hardly anyone's loyalty is guaranteed indefinitely. No matter what they tell you." Finally realizing I was also in the room, she tilted her head over her shoulder and smiled at me before returning to her conversation.

"If Greenville truly seems like the logical next step, then there's little time to waste before someone else also discovers it," Alejandra said. "Keep me updated. We may not have much time."

"Until next time, Alejandra," Gideon said. They bowed their heads toward one another before the mirror's surface began to ripple until Gideon's face was slowly replaced by Alejandra's. The world was put back in a normal, natural order if only for a short while.

"I found him," I told her. "I found Joe. In the scrying pool. He's not that far away," Alejandra beamed; a teacher taking pride in the accomplishment of her student.

"Excellent," she said, clapping her hands together. "Your adventure is just beginning. I must get you ready for the journey ahead."

She gave me a kiss on each cheek and a last-minute gift of a witch's staff. I ran my fingers along the carvings, lifted the bunch of herbs and flowers tied onto the end to inhale its sweet scent. Alejandra slipped a thin purple robe over my shoulders as I held out my arms to the side. Even without a mirror, I could still picture myself standing beside her, student and instructor.

"You have wonderful things ahead of you," Alejandra said to me. "I am absolutely certain. Know that when you return, a world of opportunity awaits. Your true fate has only just begun." A surge of unexpected emotion rushed through me. A person I've only known for little more than a month, yet she gave more than the people I've known my entire life.

"I can't thank you enough, Alejandra," I said, though those words didn't seem adequate enough to describe the extent of my gratitude. "For everything. Without you, I don't know where"

"I was only a guide," Alejandra said. "What you have done, the abilities that you have built... those are all your achievements. And I couldn't be prouder."

I wasn't ready to leave. Not yet. There was still a world of discovery waiting for me with Alejandra as my guide. What new powers would another couple of months of training grant me? Yet, there was also a part of me that tugged my body toward the door, hungry and desiring what I knew I needed to do next. It was time to flap my wings on my own for the first time, to jump from the nest and see for myself if I could fly on my own with all Alejandra taught me.

"What happens next?" I asked. "For you? After I leave?"

"I have been searching so long for a substance that can make our magic more potent," Alejandra said. I wondered if this "substance" was related to her conversations I had overhead.

"I believe that we are getting close to discovering the source of it. And when we do, I want you right there alongside me so that you can grow greater than you already have." She put a hand on my back, and we walked toward the door.

"We have such exploits waiting for us ahead when you return," she said. "Your dream will become a reality. We will make our dreams of freedom happen together." She smiled the widest that I had ever seen, her aura filled with a warm contentment. In that moment, she wasn't *malika* or a coven leader or a grand witch to me. She was just Alejandra. A mother. A teacher. The closest relationship I ever had with anyone, more of a family to me than my own flesh and blood.

She gave me one last kiss on my forehead, cradled my face in hands, and we shared one last moment.

With much longing, I tore myself away from Alejandra and looked ahead to the next part of my journey.

MY MIND FILLED with wondrous visions of the road ahead. I already knew my destination, but the path to it was filled with endless and satisfying possibilities. First step was finding Joe.

I broke in my staff when I flew to the location the scrying pool had showed me. Or rather, what I had to deduce from the smattering of images of Joe's recent travels. The city of George-town, a lower-class version of Springville, some parts of which could even be considered a slum. A big step down from where he used to live, which brought a grin to my face.

The staff granted me the power to soar invisible through the sky, powerful and free. Alejandra warned me the invisibility charm would only work for so long before I would reappear. The trip to Georgetown took only a couple of hours. When I landed, I set up my home base at a cheap motel I wouldn't have felt safe in had I been my old self. But now, with my newly developed skills, I knew the people around me were the ones who should truly be afraid.

I began staking out the places where Joe had been: a warehouse where I assumed he worked, a convenience store that he must've visited from time to time, a couple of fast-food restaurants. The scrying had given me a vision of his apartment, but nothing that was clear enough to give me a distinct address. I would have to find Joe the old-fashioned way.

For a time, I thought it wasn't going to work. I wasn't going to find Joe no matter what I did. He escaped into the ether and would never have to answer for the crimes he committed. What would I do if I couldn't find him? Would I just go back to Alejandra's empty-handed? Search for his accomplice instead?

Finally, on the evening of the third day, I spotted a familiar face going into a burger chain, one of the locales I saw reflected in the charmed pool of water. The sight of him sent a jolt of electricity through my body and my hands involuntarily curled into fists. That bastard, casually walking into the restaurant with his hands in his pockets as if he were just an ordinary guy, not even a warlock, with nothing to atone for. I bit my lip, trying to contain my knee-jerk reaction of wanting to take him down right then and there, without a care of who saw or what the consequences for that might be. I wanted to inflict tenfold the pain he and his friend had tried to impose on me. I wanted him to choke on his food. I wanted to see him helpless. I wanted to see him squirm.

He looked out of the window I was standing beside, and my heart fluttered for a moment when I thought he saw me. But then his gaze continued to wander until he received his food and headed toward the exit with a sandwich in one hand. He ate as he walked.

This was my moment. This was my time. My heart was pounding. I hid myself in a crowd of pedestrians and waited until he was about halfway down the block before I followed, being sure to keep my distance. My senses were laser-focused on him, drowning out the regular city noises I knew must have been going on around me.

After a few blocks, I realized we were across the street from the apartment building I had seen during my scrying vision.

We were almost there. I couldn't contain the smile that spread across my face.

I stood outside, out of sight, as he let himself into the building and into his apartment. From there, his second-floor apartment was visible through a window, blinds barely shut. He put his food down, turned on the TV, and grabbed a dumbbell that was on the floor. As he pumped his arm up and down, he stared at the screen with a glazed over expression. It was almost funny how little he knew his life was about to change.

The first step was getting his attention. I picked up the closest rock I could find and flung it at his window, shattering the glass. Like a reflex, he dropped the dumbbell and flattened himself against the floor.

"Who's there?" he shouted with a trembling voice, eyes darting around in search of a source he wouldn't see until I decided it was time. I walked toward the shattered window, savoring every step I took toward his frightened form, and pulled myself up on the ledge. By the time he repeated the question, I was already stepping over the windowpane into his apartment. He scrambled up from the floor and pressed himself against the wall farthest from me.

"What do you want from me?" he yelled, raising his hands up in defeat. For the first time, I saw the scarring on the flesh of his palms, with curves that suggested a symbol. The branding Alejandra previously mentioned, a way for them to be identified even if they tried to re-integrate with a coven somewhere else.

"Please, I'll give you money, anything you want," he continued. "I won't call the cops or anything. Please, just let me"

"You remember me, don't you?" I asked. As I approached

him, I savored each of his jerky motions. It didn't matter what he tried to do now. He was at my mercy.

His eyes squinted in confusion. His head shook so rapidly that the beads of sweat streaming down his forehead shook free.

"What?" he said. "No, I don't"

"You really don't remember me, Joe?" I asked him.

"H-how do you know my name?" he asked. His chest rose and sunk, rose and sunk with each shallow, panicked breath he took as I continued to approach him.

"Really, Joe? You don't remember the innocent woman that you and your friend left for dead?"

He stopped shaking. His eyes widened and lit up with a combination of fear and recognition. He rubbed his eyes with disbelief before gasping at my presence once more.

"No," he said. "No, no, no, no, it can't be you! But how did you...." He trailed off. His lips still trembling with words he was too frightened to say. His chest expanded and deflated faster with every passing moment. My heart raced with excitement as the moment I had been waiting for drew closer.

"How do you think, Joe? It's the same thing that got you into your position now. Magic."

"Magic?" he asked.

"Yes, Joe. You're not the only one with that ability." He remained still while I continued to walk toward him, only a couple of feet away.

"Please, I-I don't even mess with that shit anymore. Not since we got kicked out. I left all that behind. I can't even remember the last time I even tried to cast a spell. I've really changed. I've taken my life in a new direction. I'm-I'm sorry, okay? You've gotta believe me. Things got out of hand. We never"

"Intended for me to survive?" I asked. "I don't intend for you to survive either. Let's hope I do a better job than you did."

"Pl" was the last sound I allowed him to make before I struck out at him, slapping his face with the back of my hand. While he clutched his face, whimpering and confused, I pulled my knife out of my robe, preparing for the ritual soon to come.

He held his cheek on one of his hands, still whimpering, making sounds I couldn't interpret into words. His pain, though only an ounce of what he had inflicted, was music to my ears. I kept flashing back to that night, the way he dug into my flesh. Them laughing, confident they were going to get away with all of it, like all of this was just a game. Maybe it had been to them.

A fire raged from my navel upward, a blossoming anger invoked by his vile presence, and the recollections it brought with it.

I had the knife raised above him. He threw his hands up again in defeat, revealing his brand for a second time. I hope he was humiliated when Alejandra's coven carried out his punishment. His lips were moving but his voice was drowned out by my thoughts. But I wasn't going to kill him, not when I still had things I needed to get out of him first.

I let the knife drop to the floor, watching as his eyes followed its trajectory and he grew even more confused. So clueless.

Kneeling, I placed my hands on his shoulders, steadying his trembling body, beaming as I looked into his eyes and found fear. With an inhale, I readied myself for the next step, a feat I had not practiced since my official induction. I just needed to steady myself, remember what Alejandra and I had practiced, remind myself of how far I had come and how much I still had left to do with my mentor. I could do this.

I braced myself for the pain as I tore myself from my physical shell, yelling that turned into growling as I emerged in my new form. My old body, temporarily cast off, flopped backward onto the ground. I knew my new self was solid when I opened my eyes and saw Joe's gaping mouth and tears leaking down his face. My new form towered above him, no longer just a woman with magic. He kept staring at me, motionless. I grabbed his arms, closed my eyes, and willed myself forward into his skin.

Entering a new body for the first time felt like my entire body being shoved against a rock, sending my head spinning. I waded my way through the dizziness and disorientation, gathering and centering myself. When I came to, I clenched and unclenched the hands of my new shell. I looked around, saw my body lying on the floor, as still as a corpse. A bluish gas spread from my current shell's head to the ceiling. Joe's essence untethered from his body for the time being. Each movement I made in this new form felt foreign, but that was okay for now. I wasn't going to need this exterior for much longer.

A deluge of Joe's memories suddenly rushed into my mind. The faint visions of events that were useless to me, zipping uncontrollably past my eyelids. I stopped the stream when it came to the night of my attack, seeing everything from his twisted perspective.

Me and Seymour had just been messing around that night. He had just spotted an ordinary woman in her car, looking up at us. Our temporary invisibility spells had worn off. That night, I hadn't been quite in the mood for our usual shenanigans. I wanted to leave her alone. Seymour told me that he had other plans. He told me to lighten up and have some fun. So, I followed him. He had been right. That night had been a blast, reminding me of the good old days. Surely, more of our secret nightly adventures were to come afterward. We had been getting away with it for so long, I saw no reason why I should worry this time.

I saw the news before Seymour did. The gristly result of our nightly fun laid out in a broadcast story. The woman had been found alive. I called him, panicking, asking him what we should do because sooner or later we would be found out. He told me to calm down and relax, everything would be alright, only I couldn't understand how.

I used to think that something was wrong with me. Ever since my early days of study, I always had compulsions to hurt with my magic, to see how I could twist and contort another person's body to my will. I had kept them hidden for so long, until I had found a brother in Seymour. He and I thought in deliciously similar ways. Whenever possible, we would allow ourselves to give into our urges. Seymour helped nurture my dark side. He was the first to finally understand me.

We had always been in the business of ordinary bystanders. Mostly women. Broads were where we had the real fun. As long as they didn't survive, we were good, satisfied with the fact that the boring mundane world would never be able to discover the source of these disappearances. They would never believe that it had been warlocks.

Now that we were going to be caught, I would lose everything. All of the potential I used to have ahead of me. I was going to be a great warlock. I just needed to get this violence out of my system. I hadn't been quite there yet, but soon. I could've made it.

Alejandra, the closest thing we had to a leader, called a community meeting. She gathered all the witches and warlocks in Springfield to watch as two of her associates held Seymour and I down, forcing our palms outward so that they could burn the mark into our flesh. Seymour struggled against our captors, yelling out all kinds of obscenities, only stopping when Alejandra slapped him. She held up a staff, charmed to glow fire-red, and pressed it into my palm. I don't remember screaming, though I must have. I do remember almost passing out from the pain. When I became fully conscious again, the crowd was still around me and she had ordered our banishment.

I was completely humiliated, ex-communicated, and banished with nowhere else to turn. Among our community, news spreads fast. Seymour and I would never be able to re-integrate ourselves unless we went someplace far away, and neither of us had the funds or resources to do that. He wanted to fight against her, but even he knew that that was a stupid idea. She was far more powerful than the two of us combined. Seymour and I went our separate ways: he to a city a few hours away, and me to my current apartment. I had only gone to visit him one time since. Terrible idea. Being around him reminded me of the dark part of myself I wanted to bury. I never contacted him again after that. At least I acknowledged that we had screwed up. But Seymour just continued to curse at Alejandra and the rest of the coven in Springfield. He couldn't move on. He just couldn't let it go.

I lost my place. I didn't even want to mess with that magic shit anymore. Couldn't even remember the last time I tried to cast a puny spell. The world had discovered the darkness within me and rejected me for it. Now I would have to start from scratch, all because Seymour and I had screwed up and that broad had lived. All I wanted now was to live my life as some ordinary guy, blending into the rest of the crowd. If only she hadn't decided to pop back into my life just as I was beginning to make progress.

WITH THAT LAST THOUGHT, I wrenched myself out of his body. I went back into my own, having gotten the information I needed most from him, feeling at home within my own skin. I stood above him, waiting for something to happen. After only a few moments, the shimmering haze of his essence descended from the ceiling and crashed back into his body, jolting him awake.

"I'm-I'm *sorry*," he said. "I shouldn't have done it. I know I shouldn't have done it. I deserved to be punished. But I'm trying to make amends. You've gotta"

I pulled my knife back out to silence him.

"Make a single sound, and I will make this as painful for you as it was for me." His eyes went wide, but he did not speak a word.

I turned his TV all the way up before I got to work, slashing at his flesh to carve the appropriate symbol and watching the blood gush from him. He flailed around at first, instinctively trying to fight back. By the end, his eyes rolled up into his head and his entire body shivered. I chanted the ancient words I rehearsed that would turn his death into my power. He broke his silence and pleaded with me, asking me why I was doing this.

"It's only fair that I repay you the great favor that you did for me," I said. I took in a breath before stabbing him one last time in the chest, blood spilling everywhere, staining the carpet. His strength poured into me after I placed my palms into the puddle and lifted them up to my face, feeling his strength pour into me. A unique warmth spread through my body, restoring some of the strength my use of magic had drained. His spilled blood was so precious.

As I watched his life force leave his body, dripping out through his bloody wounds and streaming into me, I thought I had never experienced such a pleasant sensation. I soaked up the moment, savoring his spirit while I waited for his body to disintegrate into nothing, bit by bit, particle by particle.

The moment of Joe's death and mystical evaporation should have helped to quench my thirst for revenge. But killing Joe became an appetizer, a mere teaser to a greater sensation. Without looking back, I set my sights on Joe's old pal, Seymour.

My only plan with Seymour had consisted of a vague bloodlust. Joe had felt guilty, more so because he was caught than for the actual act he committed. Of the two, Seymour had been the ringleader. Seymour's end needed to be extra satisfying. Leaving Joe's apartment under the cover of night, I hopped on my staff and began the next step in my journey.

18

The high I felt from absorbing Joe's essence, that buzz, was sweeter than any drug I had ever tried. I felt like I was floating as I glided from one street to the next, savoring the tingles that ran up and down my body. I was almost in disbelief in the best way possible of what I did. One of my tormentors was no more. And even better, his buddy, Seymour, would be next. He had no idea of the fate that awaited him.

I would have loved to have made it to Seymour's direction later that night, but after traveling halfway there on my staff, I felt a heavy weight come over me. I could hardly keep my eyes open. Despite my efforts to keep myself awake, I must have passed out for just a second. When I came to, my altitude was suddenly lower and my staff was pointed in the wrong direction. My muscles felt stiff, my body sore, as if I were coming down with a fever. Alejandra taught me about this before. The *inhaka*. The inevitable exhaustion you get from using too much magic in too short of a time and shifting from one form to the next. Fighting against the parts of my heart and brain that told me to go nonstop, I decided to land for the night and check myself into a cheap hotel for a little shut-eye. I couldn't take care of Seymour, at least not in the satisfying way I had imagined, if I did not let my magic muscles heal. All I needed to do was rest for a few hours, eat a hearty meal, and be on my way.

My memories of checking into the hotel or getting into bed were a blur. The last thing I remembered was seeing, on a clock somewhere, that it was shortly past midnight. But when I awoke the next day, I immediately checked the clock and saw that it was now almost 1 p.m. When I stood up and stretched my limbs, I felt refreshed. A small fog hung at the back of my head, but it was nothing I couldn't handle. I yawned and readied myself. Today was the day, and now was the time.

IT WAS the evening by the time I arrived in Seymour's city. While scanning his pathetic memories, Joe gave me some other crucial information about Seymour I would use to my benefit. He thought of himself as a womanizer, a mini Casanova, even with a girlfriend in his life, and he could not resist the charms of a busty redhead. My hair color was the wrong shade for his taste, but I held the power to change that.

I walked around in search of someone who could fit the description. Wandering around, I finally found a woman that fit the description. She slid out of her car onto the sidewalk, staring down at her phone, unaware of her surroundings. I followed her until she rounded a corner into an alleyway between two buildings, still paying the rest of the world no mind.

"*Alama*," I whispered, aiming at her right arm, sneaking behind her. She jumped from the burst of pain, dropping her phone. From there, it was all too easy to cover her mouth and will out of my body into hers. I carried my shell to her car, heaving it into the backseat, and drove it to the woman's house.

I placed it inside for safekeeping. The location of her house was revealed to me during the flood of her uninteresting memories.

Joe's memories pointed me to the approximate neighborhood in which Seymour resided. I drove to the proper intersection and parked on a nearby curb. I hopped out and continued my journey on foot, paying attention to each house I passed in search of the right one.

I hadn't even gotten to Seymour's house, but I was already feeling some satisfaction from my new shell. I was bracing the streets with my presence, gathering stares from passersby. As I searched for his house, it started raining, making my plan that much better. Lots of rain made for wet clothes, damp hair, and sparkling eyes. I went from gorgeous to stunning.

Something about the block I stumbled on tugged at me with its familiarity. My heart began to race, warming my extremities that had been chilled by the frosty rain. With each step I took, the sense of familiarity grew, coming to a head when I found myself standing in front of an otherwise nondescript house I had seen from Joe's perspective. I planted my feet firmly on the ground and clenched my fists before setting foot on his doorstep. I braced myself for whatever emotions might arise from seeing the ringleader again.

The sadness those memories used to invoke had now been rubbed smooth and all that remained was anger. A desire to right what they had tried to destroy. Joe hadn't stood a chance. He didn't even try to use any magic against me. Had it been shock? A lack of practice? In his last moments, he accepted death as his only option. Maybe he wanted me to put his pathetic life out of misery.

After so many weeks of training, the final moment was about to arrive. The anger and eagerness propelled me forward.

I raised my clenched fist and knocked on the door.

When Seymour answered on the second knock, the torrent of emotions almost knocked me over. I was shocked standing face to face with my attacker after so much time passed. I had a moment of fear as I remembered my old self's powerlessness. That was replaced with the burning flame of anger, a crushing desire to stomp him into the pavement outside right then and there. *All in due time*, I thought to myself. I forced my mouth into a friendly grin.

Joe cared enough to change his appearance since the attack. Seymour didn't. He looked as awful as before, like no time had passed, like he hadn't been exiled from his community for the rest of his life.

I realized that he was staring back at me with wonder.

"Who are you?" he asked me. I pushed away the fear his voice had once caused and instead drew upon every lusty stereotype I could think of to create another persona. I pursed my lips, attempting to sound as stupid and sultry as I could.

"I'm lost," I said, drawing out each letter to full effect.

"Lost?" he asked, staring at my lips. I slowly nodded.

"My car broke down. And now I'm soaking. Can you believe it?" His eyes dropped down from my face to my breasts and beyond. I could have been threatening his life and he still would have been too distracted to do anything.

"Can I use your phone? Mine is all out of charge." He gulped and then stared at me like he was about to drool, finally nodding his head and stepping aside to allow me to set foot into his home.

"So, uh, what's your name?" he asked as he closed the door.

"Gina," I said, coming up with the name on a whim. When I turned around to look at him, his drooling expression gave me little reason to think my false name had tipped him off to anything odd. He obviously wasn't thinking with the head on his shoulders. Playing up my lustfulness a bit more seemed like a great idea.

I wrapped my arms around myself and pretended to shiver. Seymour instantly attended to me. He stepped toward me, placed a hand on my shoulder like he was capable of being a genuinely concerned person.

"What's wrong?" he asked.

"I'm just cold," I said. "Cold and wet. Can I use your phone? I'll be out of here in no time."

"My phone?" he asked. His eyes dropped down to my chest again.

"Your phone," I repeated.

"Yeah, my phone. I can get that for you."

He ran out of the room and disappeared from my sight. While he was gone, I glanced around his living room, looking for anything that could prove useful or anything that could give me a potential advantage in our upcoming encounter. All I found was a row of photos hanging on his wall of him and his girlfriend, to whom he had no problem being unfaithful to. Just an ordinary house, no sign of magic or the supernatural anywhere. Had he abandoned the craft just as his accomplice had, moving onto more mundane terrors?

I wasn't staring at his photos for even a minute when I found myself being pushed to the floor, landing flat on my stomach so I couldn't see my attacker. Seymour had come up behind me and held both of my wrists in one of his hands in a painful, vice-like grip, using his other hand to pin my neck down.

Seymour had taken me by surprise for the very last time.

"You will do as I say," he said. His mouth was right next to my right ear. "Otherwise, I will make you realize that I am capable of doing things that will make you wish you hadn't come here in the first place. Do you understand me?"

His words wished to frighten me, but I already promised myself I would never let this man scare me again. Instead, his words acted like gasoline poured into the fire of anger that engulfed me, igniting my muscles and every inch of my skin.

"Do you understand me?" he repeated louder this time, spitting into my ear.

I grinned and retreated into myself in concentration, picturing his hands as clearly as I could.

"*Alama*," I said. He yelped and let go of my wrists, jumping away from me like he had been shocked by electricity. I pushed myself back up to stand and stared him down while he tried to gather himself.

"What the hell?" he shouted. "What is going on?" He looked down at his hands, which had been burned and scarred just like Joe's.

"Who the hell are you?" he said, clenching his hands into fists, coming toward me. I readied myself to counter whatever his next move was going to be.

"*Hariyak!*" he shouted. Two small streams of fire erupted from his hands. Since I was able to jump away just in time, the flames slightly singed some of my skin and dress. I barely noticed the pain.

"Maybe it's been a while since I used this, but I'll be damned if I let all those years of training go to waste," he said. "Now, I'll give you one last chance to answer me, and maybe this won't end with you dead. Who the hell are you? Why are you here? Did that bitch, Alejandra, send you? I guess public shaming wasn't enough of a punishment for her."

"Do you really not recognize me?" I asked. "Not even in this form? You didn't think that the name I gave you was a bit odd?"

"Look, why don't you just leave right now before things get really nasty?" He raised a hand toward me as he slowly walked forward, poised to throw some other magical obstacle at me.

"No, that's the not the way that this works. I'm not going to just walk away and forget after what you did to me."

"What are you" He quickly shut his mouth.

"Dina," he said, shaking his head in disbelief, sounding more surprised than scared. I was about to change that.

"You were right about one thing," I said. "I didn't think that exile was a harsh enough punishment."

"I don't know how you're suddenly casting spells, but I've been training for a lifetime," he said. "Whatever little puny charm you try to throw at me won't do a damn thing. I'm only going to warn you one last time to walk away, right now. Whatever you're trying to do here is pointless. I almost killed you once; I can sure as hell do the deed again. Except this time, I'll do it right."

"Pointless?" I asked. "Really?" My momentary hesitation gave him the opportunity to gain the upper hand.

"You think you're so powerful now?" he said, continuing to creep forward. "You're just as helpless as you were before. I can already see the seed of darkness growing within you. Killing me isn't going to make that go away. You'll never escape being our little victim. We should have crushed you while we had the chance." His little speech caught me off guard. He came toward me faster than I could react and grabbed my throat with his hand, looking dead into my eyes. All I could see was the darkness that existed within him alone that I would soon vanquish from existence.

"I don't know how you found this new body, but rest assured, it's not going to make it through the night," he said.

As he choked me, I used the last of my breath to whisper *Alama*. He didn't fully let go of me this time but loosened his grip enough for me to breathe and fight back. I held out my hand to recite the word that would make him lie still for a few seconds. *Sokara*. The same method he once used on me now froze him in his current position.

Seymour began reciting something unknown to me as soon as the "s" slipped from my lips. Immediately afterward, a force came from my right side and knocked me onto the floor. An invisible attacker, no doubt summoned by Seymour, that he had waited until this moment to unleash. It did not remain invisible to me for long. I could see the faintest whisper of smoke hanging in the air, the physical manifestation of whatever ethereal spell Seymour had invoked for his protection.

Seymour came at me again, his eyes twinkling with thirst. If I had indeed been his last attempted sacrifice, then it would have been months since he last indulged in his dark desires. He'd been waiting for so long to find his next source of prey to fulfill his thirst. This was all probably just a game to him, another power fantasy. Another woman to slaughter to fulfill his taste for blood. How many other sacrifices had he and Joe made? How many more women would have died at his hand had I not survived?

I snapped myself out of that train of thought, realizing I had little time to think of my next action. It was time for me to let go of this pretty girl persona and release the monster within me.

The pain of emerging from my shell seemed to shrink each time I carried it out. It wasn't so much that the discomfort itself went away, but I knew it was only temporary. I was strong enough to withstand the physical sensation after all I had already endured. I told myself this as I imagined myself tearing through the body of this beautiful redhead.

With the painful part over, I was finally free.

My encounter with Joe didn't produce as much satisfaction I was experiencing now, standing above Seymour, and watching the smugness drip away from his face while he looked at my new form. He was shocked; he couldn't move. The moment of fear when his face fell, realizing he was no longer the grand ringmaster of the show, proved he truly had no idea what he was up against. He thought a beginner witch with some introductory knowledge of spells was no match for him. But a mythical creature sprang to life right before his eyes. I don't think his mind was able to comprehend.

"You bitch!" he yelled. "We should have killed you when we had the chance!"

Seymour regained some of his previous focus, scrambling to his feet, tossing spells at me; bursts of pain, flame, ice, spells meant to slice the flesh. None of his recitations were enough to keep me down for long while he tried to clamber his way to the nearby kitchen. I used one of my claws to strike him against the wall. His head hit the wall with a satisfying thud I hoped cracked his skull. He touched the back of his head and then looked down at his hands, expecting blood, before returning to his previously unsuccessful attempt to magic his way out of this.

If I had been a normal body, in any other setting, his spells would have been enough to incapacitate me, even kill me. But then, with my anger and adrenaline soaring to new heights, nothing could keep me from moving toward my goal. My mind barely registered any of the pain or damage being done to my new grotesque figure while I chased him around the house from room to room. Unfazed by any of Seymour's actions, I clawed him a few times before letting him escape just to see him double over in pain before gathering himself and trying to run away again in desperation. He tried hiding behind an open door or within a closet, but his trail of dripping blood kept me on his tail.

As I chased him, his spells grew weaker and his energy drained from not having practiced magic in so long. He somehow found the energy to yell threats at me. His threats softened with his increasing fatigue and frustration until the only noise he made was panicked breathing. When I cornered him in a bedroom upstairs, I found him lying on the ground; his eyes were brimming with fear while he panted and bled profusely. His shirt was practically torn to shreds, and what little fabric remained was stained red. Rivers of blood flowed down his arms and his legs, his face coated in the glistening liquid. He clutched his abdomen, the site of a large, bleeding gash. His chest rose and fell irregularly. I knew it wouldn't be long until the deed was done.

"You're a lot harder to kill than Joe was," I said. He couldn't have hidden the surprise in eyes if he tried.

"You killed Joe?" he asked. His breathing grew more troubled, and his eyes became glassy. He shut his eyes and groaned while he shifted positions. The action seemed to use up most of what little life force remaining.

"What Joe and I did was wrong," he began, panting between words. "Sick and terrible. But what you're about to do to me is also terrible." He crumpled up his face like he was the undeserving, innocent victim. I did not believe his sincerity for even a moment. When I looked at his face and into his eyes, all I saw were black holes filled with more lies. An evil that killed countless others and would have carried on killing if someone didn't put a stop to it.

"I don't believe you, Seymour," I said. My voice was far more demanding in this form than it could have ever been in my previous body. "You tried to attack me again, and now you're begging for your life. Only because you're scared to die. You're not sorry about what you did. You're just sorry that I lived."

The Seymour I had come to expect suddenly took back over as he dropped the masquerade and his face fell into a slick smile.

"Maybe you're right," he said, trying to sound like a badass despite still having to take deep breaths in between words. "I don't feel the least bit bad about what I did. I enjoyed it. We made you, Dina. You wouldn't be what you are now without us."

I lunged toward Seymour and grabbed his chest with my clawed fist, heaving him up on the wall above me. His face was filled with terror while shouting at me to put him back down. He thought his speech would catch me off guard, giving him the chance to gain the upper hand again. No such luck for him.

"You didn't make me into anything," I said. "You tried to crush me. But that's all in the past. You no longer have any control over me. You want to know who helped me become this? Alejandra. The same woman who took everything away from you. But you, Seymour, don't have control over anything. Not even yourself." I squeezed into his chest a little, letting his blood flow like raindrops, watching his face contort with pain.

"Your time has come," I said.

I pulled my claw from his chest and threw him onto the floor. He did not move. The only sign he was still alive was the slow rise and fall of his diminishing breathing. I started chanting the sacred words, using one of my claws to carve the symbols into his flesh. He was quiet at the beginning, trying to be strong and stubborn and not reveal any of his pain. By the time I finished the proper rites, he was screaming just as much as I had, squirming to get away but not having the strength to move his body. Even when the circle was cast, Seymour still jerked around like a worm, refusing to accept his fate.

I leaned over him, looked into the dark holes of his terrified, helpless eyes, and swiped a single claw across his neck. He gurgled, raising his arms to try to wrap his hands around his throat as the red ribbon blossomed from the gash. I stepped away to admire my work as Seymour's body released the last of his blood.

When his arms dropped down to his sides and he stopped moving, I was able to catch another glimpse of the branded mark of exile he and Joe shared, scarred over and now soaked in blood. I reveled in the ruby pool around his blood, much like I had with Joe's, feeling my strength grow with each passing moment as the ritual took hold. The distinct warmth coursed through my body, filling me with a satisfaction that made me want to sing with delight. Nothing could match my rush. I was the most powerful being in the world, even in the universe.

As I sat there patiently waiting for Seymour's body to

dissolve drop by drop, I let the reality of what I accomplished flow over me. I defeated the last of the two warlocks who brought on the darkest days of my life. I had, in turn, become far stronger than they could ever be. Returning to my old body could bring me down. It was just a shell. No matter what form I took, the fact remained I had taken on my attackers against all odds and emerged victorious.

I had fulfilled my purpose.

All I had to do now was return home.

19

———

The house my sister and I once shared seemed so small now compared to the vast world I was introduced to over the past few months. Clad in my robes, and carrying my staff in my left hand, I walked down the once familiar sidewalk to the place that was my own form of prison.

I could have, and should have, gone straight to Alejandra's after I was done with Seymour. But on my way back to Greenfield, something kept nagging at me. I needed to cut the last remaining ties to my old life. That Dina was gone. I couldn't be sure what Kayla's reaction would be and hoped that her joy at seeing me again would be enough to eclipse whatever she felt regarding my disappearance and sudden reappearance.

I straightened up my spine, recalling the confidence and sense of achievement I felt immediately after confronting Joe and Seymour. What I was about to do was nothing compared to what I already accomplished. Pushing aside my hesitance, I knocked on the door.

Kayla's familiar face emerged in the door frame. A face so like mine, yet dissimilar enough to relay the differences between us. There was my older sister, an emerging talent, a small-time actress and singer headed for stardom. And then there was me, who despite my best, couldn't seem to do anything of significance in my old life. But what I knew now was that I wasn't stuck with this body. I could become whoever I wanted with the right shell.

We stood, staring at each other, motionless and silent for a few seconds. It felt like lifetimes while I waited for her to speak. She blinked in disbelief and then threw her arms around.

"Dina," she said. "Dina, I can't believe it's you!" She pulled me inside, shutting the door behind her.

"I just-wow," she said. I took a seat at our dining room table, setting down my staff and leaning it on the side of my chair. She paced around, running her hands through her hair. "I don't even know what to say." She took a seat across from me and stared at me again. Though the place was familiar, the emotions I felt were not. I didn't understand my presence there anymore. I felt too much like I was trying to force myself into a home where I never really belonged. I had no need for this place anymore.

"Where on earth have you been?" she asked. Before I could answer, she pulled her cellphone from her pocket and furiously began to type.

"Kayla, what are you doing?" I asked.

"Calling Mom and Dad," she said. "They'll be so happy to find out" I laid a hand over her arm.

"Please, don't do that. Not now. Not yet."

She set her phone down and wiped her face with her hands. I hadn't realized she was crying when she was on her phone. She reached across the table and my hands into hers.

"We were so, so worried about you," she told me. "All of us. We thought you might've been dead, Dina." She squeezed my hands, and more tears ran down her face.

"But the letter I sent you. Didn't you get that?"

"Of course, I did. But we were still so worried! Don't you

understand that, Dina? You had that horrible thing happen to you and then you suddenly went missing! Where were you all this time? How could you just send us a letter without even telling us where you had gone? Mom and Dad...we even tried to file a missing person's report. But the office here didn't take it seriously; they all thought that you had run off on your own. We had no idea that" She closed her eyes shut as another jet of tears trickled down her cheeks.

"I'm sorry, Kayla," I said, feeling my eyes watering up. "But I just couldn't stay here anymore. You understand that, right? I needed to get away from here and"

"Without telling me?" she interrupted. "Without telling any of us? How could you not expect us to worry? Mom and Dad know all about your evening wanderings and how you used to talk to yourself at night. We didn't know how much pain you were in. We didn't even know how much we would be able to help. All we really wanted was for you to get the help and care that you needed. None of us could"

It was my turn to interrupt.

"But I did, Kayla. I did get help. The best help that I could find." She shook her head in confusion.

"I don't understand," she said. "Why didn't you just tell us? If you checked yourself into a hospital, you know that Mom and Dad could've-"

"I didn't go to any hospital," I said. "It's not like any of them would believe me anyway."

"Then where did you go?" she asked. I hesitated on whether I should even bother telling her the truth, or if it would just be a waste of my breath. I reminded myself of why I came here, and what I needed to do before going back to Alejandra's to resume my adventure into my new world.

"I was training. To become a witch." Kayla squinted her eyes and stared at me, loosening her grip on my hands.

"The men who did this to me were warlocks. They tried to

sacrifice me, Kayla, that's what the attack was. But it gave me new abilities. I've been in this city this entire time. This wonderful woman, Alejandra, helped me with everything." I paused, waiting for her to say something or at the very least have some sort of reaction. I cut myself off without bothering to explain my forays into blood magic or revenge. I was unsure of how she would handle those topics after the introduction I just gave her.

Kayla pulled her hands away from mine, looked down at the table, and shook her head.

"All I wanted was the truth, Dina," she said.

"But I am telling you the truth," I said. "I didn't think you would believe me anyway, but this is what has happened. I've made sense of everything that has happened to me. Do you know how that feels, Kayla? After being in pain for so long?" She looked back up from the table, and all I saw was the same disappointment our parents used to look at me with.

"Dina, I don't know where you went, and at this point, I'm not going to keep asking. You're not well. It's been several months, and you're still not well. We're all really worried about you. We really want you to get better. That's why I need to call Mom and Dad. We can get you to"

"But I am better, Kayla!" I yelled. "I know it's hard for you to understand, but I am so much better than I have ever been." I knew I should've given up trying to convince her of anything, yet something in me still wanted to fight. No one else would be able to force their version of Dina onto me.

"We need to get out of here," she said. "This town is going downhill. There's been so much crime lately. You're not safe in the streets. You're not even safe in your own home. Murders are happening left and right. A house got burned down just the other day. People keep getting robbed. Someone even tried to break into our home here when you were away. They don't seem to ever catch the criminals, either. It's like no one is safe here anymore. Mom and Dad invited me to live back home. You can come with me. We'll all be together, and we can get you the care that you need. I've been reading while you were gone. I understand that this...fantasy of yours might be a coping mechanism, but..." It was if she hadn't heard a single word that I had said. I thought back to the night where we witnessed an otherworldly creature emerging from my bedroom mirror, and her refusal to accept what she saw with her own eyes. There was no getting through to her. I felt so stupid and foolish for even having thought that coming here was a good idea. It might have been better if I remained *missing* and let Kayla and our parents fill in the rest of the story for themselves.

I broke myself out of my old thinking patterns, reminding myself there was no need to stay here. No one, not Kayla, not our mother, not our father, determined what I did next with my life. I could leave if I wanted to. I stood up, grabbed my staff, and prepared to do just that.

"Dina," Kayla said, jumping up from the table. "Dina, where are you going?"

"I only came to say goodbye," I said. "You won't have to worry about me anymore." I wrapped my arms around, giving her a hug that she did not reciprocate. I fought back tears when I turned around to face the door.

"What do you mean!" she shouted. "You can't just leave again! Just stay for a little bit longer. I'll call Mom and Dad and then we can..." I tuned her out and continued my path to the front door. Kayla continued trailing behind me. She was pleading with me not to go, repeating about how we could all be together as a family. How I didn't need to go off on my own anymore, that she would listen to my story about where I had been if I sat down and waited for our parents to get there. I fought back tears when I walked through the door. Kayla walked behind me, calling one of our parents and shouting about how I was back and about to leave again. I was too afraid to turn back around and let her see me crying.

We came to a road with oncoming traffic. I bolted across it as quickly as I could. Kayla was not fast enough to keep up with me. As the cars rushed between us, I kept sprinting, putting more distance between us until I was confident I was far enough away.

Despite my tears, I knew this was the way I needed to go. They would be better off without the *blemish* of my existence they perceived me as. I needed to continue becoming the Dina I was always meant to be.

MY HEART RACED with excitement when I approached Alejandra's house. The conversation with my sister was a sidebar for the real moment when I returned home. I felt confident with my decision regarding my family, and everything involved with letting go of my old life. That Dina was gone now, and my old life had no place in the world of magic I was discovering. I was enlarging my universe and the limits of what I thought was possible. I couldn't wait to see my mentor again to tell her all I did and move onto the next stage of our adventures with her by my side.

When I walked the path to her house, it became increasingly obvious something wasn't right. Even from afar, I could see hints of destruction that awaited me. I ran the remaining block down to the house, fearful that something was wrong, and my presence was needed. The degree of destruction was not fully revealed until I stood in front of the carnage surrounded by yellow tape.

The grand estate I had come to see as my home no longer existed. What stood before me now was a shell of a house, burned to a jagged crisp; the outer walls scorched with the remnants of a fire. Alejandra's once secure home, my castle of comfort, was now revealed for anyone to enter. I could have stood there for days staring into the devastation, trying to make some sense of it, but my mind refused to believe what my eyes were seeing. I jumped to the worst of possibilities as I walked from one side of the house to another.

What happened to Alejandra? Was she still inside? Even if her house was burned down, that didn't mean anything bad happened to her, right? She could be somewhere else right now, being as potent as she had always been. She just hadn't been able to contact me in time. Maybe she left a message for me somewhere inside, directions of where to meet her next. I ignored the yellow tape and got closer to the house to begin my search.

When I looked on the back wall, where Alejandra had once invited me into her home for refuge, my illusion fell to pieces. My heart sank into my stomach. There, etched in the wall, I caught sight of a message indeed, but not one that Alejandra had left for me.

We are the force of justice.
Those who do not follow will be punished.
No matter the transgression.
Alejandra has fallen.
You must change your ways.
You have received your warning.

Alejandra. Alejandra had fallen. Her house burned down. She was gone. I dropped down to my knees as the news rolled over me. My throat closed, and the tears rushed into my eyes.

Alejandra was gone.

20

"Well, the short of it is that she was murdered," the woman told me. She was a kind old lady who happened to be a nearby neighbor. She found me in fetal position in front of the burnt shell of the house. She said that she heard the noise of someone "weeping" outside. I hadn't even realized I was making so much noise. She generously took me inside and offered me some tea and cookies, though I couldn't bring myself to ingest any of it.

I stared at my reflection in the light brown pool of tea, still swirling from the spoonful of sugar she added. Why couldn't I use it as a scrying pool to find Alejandra wherever she was now? Would it be possible for me to find her, even if it were in the afterlife, or some other dimension I had yet to discover?

"But I don't understand. Alejandra always had defenses up. She hardly ever let anyone into her house. How could this happen? I thought she was the leader around here. People followed her. Why would anyone want to do this?"

"About a day ago, a crowd swarmed outside of her house." She stirred sugar into her cup of tea as she spoke. "It was like they came from nowhere. There wasn't enough time for anyone to do anything, and there's plenty of magic folk in this neighborhood. The next thing I know, they had dragged Alejandra's body outside and destroyed what was left of her. I don't know how they did it. She was one of the strongest witches I knew. And then they burned her house right down and destroyed everything in it. Before we knew it, they were gone. They must've taken the daughter, too. There's been no trace of her ever since."

"Who did this?" I asked. She took a sip of her tea before continuing.

"I've just heard rumors, that's all," she said, setting her cup back down. "No one really seems to know who they really are. Not anyone I've spoken to, anyway. I've heard mumblings here and there about some kind of vigilante group, occasional murders happening here and there. They supposedly claim that they're taking down people who have committed 'transgressions of magic'. Whatever that is really supposed to mean. Who knows if that was really why they took her down. When you're in the kind of business that Alejandra was in, you make as many enemies as you do friends. Who knows if she really committed any kind of 'transgression'? Someone probably just wanted her power, is all. The fighting has been getting worse lately. Something like this was bound to happen sooner or later."

Transgressions of magic? I thought again about the strange and unexplained sounds I heard while in Alejandra's house. Her cryptic conversations. The strange creature she revealed to me that she said she couldn't show anyone else because it might be considered forbidden. The strange behavior of her daughter. My mind was swimming with confusion. The tears left my eyes in big, heaving globs. I refused to believe she was dead. She always seemed too powerful to be brought down by something as ordinary and human as death.

"Are you okay, honey?" the woman asked me. I shook my

head. I tried to speak but all that came out were blubbering noises from my lips drenched in tears.

"Take your time," she told me. "It seems like you and her were close, and I am so sorry for the loss that you are experiencing right now. The grief will get easier, but first you have to allow yourself to feel what you are feeling now, or you won't be able to move forward."

"I can't go home," I said. "I don't-I don't *have* a home anymore."

"You're free to stay until morning if you need it," she said.

I accepted her offer. With the way my mind was swirling with chaos, failing to accept what I saw right before me, I wasn't in any state to go anywhere. She led me to her guest room. Even cradled in covers, I still couldn't get rid of the chill that sent shivers over my body. I stared at the wall, wishing for the darkness of sleep.

Alejandra was dead. Even though I replayed the thought in my mind, it still refused to sink in and become a part of my reality. I was never going to be able to tell her about my success or have her teach me more of her ways. I was truly alone, and even more uncertain and fearful for my future. I had no idea where to go from here.

I LEFT the woman's house the following morning without a plan for what I was going to do next. Despite my confidence in my decisions just a day prior, which seemed like half a lifetime ago, when I walked alone through the city, I suddenly found myself veering from one place to the next. I played the same thoughts of grief and disbelief on loop in my head.

For the first time, I felt physical exhaustion from my adventures pressing down upon every inch of my body, the fogginess in my mind and achy muscles screaming with every step. A drowsiness that no amount of sleep could cure. With my vial of healing potion all gone, all I could do was endure and wait out the suffering.

When the pain within me grew until I was barely able to stand, I sought refuge on a bench, laying my face into my hands. My life felt like it was ending before I found Alejandra. But with her help, everything was going so much better than I could ever have imagined. And now, hit with the ultimate whammy, I couldn't see a path for what I was supposed to do next. Without a home and without Alejandra, I was lost. In my fatigued state, I didn't know if it would be possible to go on.

When my exhaustion lifted just a bit, I got up and continued to wander from one spot to another, hoping to find an answer to help me guide my future.

I shouldn't have been surprised when my wandering eventually led me back to Alejandra's house.

When I returned to my most recent home, I waded through the rubble, retracing those familiar paths I took so many mornings before. What little was left of the walls and floors was covered with soot, as if this vigilante group had been trying to cleanse the house of something, perhaps Alejandra's presence. I picked up whatever scraps I could find; burnt corners of books, a piece of her charred dining room table, and singed bits of unknown material. I needed to collect as many pieces as possible of her.

I carefully descended through a hole in the floor into the dark basement, the site of so many important events for me, illuminated only by the daylight that shone through a hole. I laid down and sprawled out in all directions, searching for another piece of her presence. When one of my fingers felt a lump of something unknown lying on the ground, I stretched out until I could grasp it. Satisfied with my collection, I heaved myself up into the floor above. Now standing in daylight, I held out the object in my hands toward the sun.

The item I discovered was a heart-shaped locket with an "A" carved into the front and an "E" carved into the back. A small cursive inscription dated it to 1948.

The locket opened with minimal effort. One side held a tiny black and white photograph of a couple whom I had never seen. The other side held a few tightly coiled blonde, almost white, hairs. I closed the locket and clasped it around my neck. A small, personal trinket to remember my mentor. With the locket now a part of my person, I gave the house one last look before walking back out into the city, sitting on the edge of night.

Somewhere during my wandering, my sadness crossed the threshold into anger, and my heart swelled with purpose. I began to understand I was nowhere close to being done with magic or revenge. It didn't matter how powerful these vigilantes thought they were. They had no idea what they had taken from me and what I would give them in return.

When I used to look upon this city, I had only felt jealousy. There were so many beautiful people trying to achieve some measure of success, living lives that I could not. Good fortune that I was so close to having but was never meant to possess. Now, I looked at all these people and saw only the fantastic possibilities their bodies could hold for my own life. I was free to leave this old body in pursuit of something better.

All I had to do was wait until the right tall blonde passed me, tear myself out of my body for the final time and leave my old, useless self behind in a crumpled heap. I was finally free. I allowed the sudden stream of boring memories into my mind. I processed them and gained the knowledge of the life of whoever this woman used to be. Whoever she had been... she was me now.

I am the newest addition to your community of magic.

I am a student who lost her teacher.

To the group that killed Alejandra, wherever you are, I will find you and make you pay for your "transgressions". You have my word.

You have received your warning.

Khalas.

READING GROUP DISCUSSION QUESTIONS

1. How do you think Dina's story will continue?
2. What are your impressions of the magic world?
3. Is Alejandra trustworthy?
4. Why do you think Joe did not fight back against Dina?
5. Why is the series called "Kindred"?
6. Would you have followed your companion wherever it led you? Or would you have been more cautious?
7. What are your thoughts about Lisa, Alejandra's daughter?
8. Which aspect of the magic system or magical being was the most interesting?

ABOUT THE AUTHOR

Zed Amadeo is an author of dark fantasy and horror, including the "Kindred" series of dark urban fantasy books. She has always held a curiosity for the unexplained and believes that every good story starts with "What If?". Zed resides in her adopted hometown of Louisville, Kentucky, where she spends far too much time watching horror movies and consuming the best works of fantasy and science fiction she can find, all of which refill her creative well and inspire her writing. When not writing or reading, Zed is a fan of day-long video game marathons, head-banging to 80s music, and connecting with other artists and creators in the speculative fiction world.

Visit Zed Amadeo's website: ZedAmadeo.com

facebook.com/zedamadeo
instagram.com/zed.amadeo

NEW SCI-FI FANTASY
FROM WAHIDA CLARK PRESENTS
INNOVATIVE PUBLISHING
LONERS
DB BRAY & WAHIDA CLARK
EMPERORS & ASSASSINS
WAHIDA CLARK
RESURRECTION
BOOK ONE IN THE KINDRED SERIES
ZED AMADEO
Fractured Princess
DEBRA RENEE BYRD
THE ROAD TO RESISTANCE
FIRST BOOK OF THE VANGUARD I
CHASE BOLLING
THE ROAD TO RESISTANCE
FIRST BOOK OF THE VANGUARD I
CHASE BOLLING
THE WAR WE MAKE
FIRST BOOK OF THE VANGUARD II
CHASE BOLLING

SFFS
SCIENCE FICTION FANTASY
FOR THE CULTURE
W. CLARK PUBLISHING

WAHIDA CLARK
PRESENTS
INNOVATIVE PUBLISHING